Laura Fedora

Robert Brancatelli

Blumen Publishing
New York

For Daniella, another redheaded girl

You must have a little patience. I have undertaken, you see, to write not only my life, but my opinions also; hoping and expecting that your knowledge of my character, and of what kind of a mortal I am, by the one, would give you a better relish for the other....and as we jog on, either laugh with me, or laugh at me, or in short, do any thing,--only keep your temper.

--O, ye critics! will nothing melt you?

Laurence Sterne
The Life and Opinions of Tristram Shandy, Gentleman, 1759

The author would like to thank Sankee Maringanti for her critique and evaluation of parts of the manuscript and Michael Carney for his gracious technical assistance. Their help was invaluable in lending authenticity to the time period and Richard's character. The author would also like to acknowledge and thank Blumen Publishing's editorial staff for their tireless efforts in getting this book out the door, especially Cynthia Sax, Tom Arbuthnot, and Marilyn Mangini, who told the author not to let the door hit him in the a--! It was also Marilyn's suggestion that, "Wipe that smirk off your face!" be included in the final draft. Finally, the author is very appreciative of you, the reader, for suspending all disbelief and stepping courageously into Mercurioland. Someday, there may even be a theme park.

R. Brancatelli,
December 2013

The package was waiting for him when he got back to his cell. It was torn from its long journey and wrapped in a brown grocery bag with his mother's return address. She had sent it to the firm in Philadelphia, and somebody there forwarded it to the jail in Belize. Inside was a finely-woven, linen greeting card with a watercolor sailboat that read, "Richard, found these during my move to Sandy Shore in Atlantic City. Thought you'd want to see them. Enjoy the memories and pray for your decrepit mother who has to have hip replacement surgery (with a two-thousand dollar deductible)!" Obviously, somebody had helped her write it, her English spelling and grammar still bearing the imprint of her native Hungary, and Richard wondered whether it was her friend at the retirement community, that slick but friendly annuities salesman from Cape May, New Jersey. The guy loved clam fritters. Richard had met him at a Sunday brunch and caught him giving his mother the eye. With any luck maybe she would give him *her* clam fritter and he would offer to pay the deductible.

The rest of the package contained report cards from elementary school, discolored Polaroids of him and his brother, Kornél, posing in front of their garage door like squinting garden gnomes, mementoes from a family trip to Hershey Park, Pennsylvania, an embarrassing napkin holder he had made in eighth-grade wood shop, and a red leather journal from high school. He recognized the journal immediately and took it out, running his fingers over the delicate fleur-de-lis design. He opened it and smelled inside. He hadn't seen it since high school, when he had handed it over to his mother for safekeeping, unable to write another word. She had placed it on the bottom shelf of the china cabinet next to the porcelain figurines from Hungary. For the longest time he had hoped that the memory of that summer in 1976 might stay locked up like those figurines. And it did up till now, when it all came back in the smell of worn leather and mold.

It was odd that ever since his arrest and incarceration in Ambergris Caye for drug trafficking—a ridiculous charge made even more so by the additional charge of attacking a constable with a "weapon" (a rusty fishing spear he had picked up while hiding from the police in a green shed at the end of the dock with a dark Mayan woman he had come to love and a back-stabbing friend and colleague he had learned to hate, but that was another story—there was always another story)—he had had nothing but time to think about time. And he did. The past mainly, which was his pastime and obsession. Some people had golf with plaid pants; others had scuba diving with masks, fins, boots, regulators, gauges, reels, and weights. It kept them occupied, he guessed. What kept him occupied was the past, which had its own version of reels and weights to keep him submerged. And although he hadn't counted the years, months, or days since high school, it made perfect sense that this journal should show up now, making its way into his life at a time when time had become meaningless, when there was nothing left for him to do but bake in the heat like leaves of tobacco. In jail, there was no time, no addition, only subtraction from the possibility of something else that would never occur.

He tucked the journal under his arm and went out to the exercise yard, resting under the sprawling breadfruit tree with massive fruit called a *mazapan*. One other inmate was there, an older Garífuna man with close-cropped, curly white hair everybody called "Junior," who had been arrested for stealing costume jewelry from one of the boutiques in town. Junior nodded in his direction and dozed back to sleep, which was how he spent most of the day. Richard looked up through the leafy branches of the tree at the cracked cement wall that enclosed the yard and the thin blue sky beyond. On the other side, tourists were running around in pastel-colored sportswear and sandals, dining on boiled lobster, conch soup, and Belikin beer while he sat here with his life in ruins. What had happened, exactly? He could barely remember. What he did remember was that he had lost everything on this trip through Central America: his job, his career, his reputation, and his freedom. As if that weren't enough, he had been waiting for months either to be charged by the public prosecutor, a lazy man with an even lazier eye who brought his perfumed wife to their meetings (it must have counted as a date), or extradited in handcuffs back to Guatemala. Sure, the charge was bogus, but trying to prove that wouldn't be easy. Nothing on this trip had been easy.

He drummed his fingers on the journal and actually thought about not reading it, not exposing himself to yet another example of failure, this one being the earliest. But he always did that, always started out on the opposite side of where he really wanted to be. Was it a diversionary tactic or a way of protecting himself? It could have been both, or maybe it was a vestige of his legal training. Admittedly, he was genetically disposed to it; being an asshole was part of his DNA. He had discovered it in earnest in law school when he had given a friend false information about a Remedies final for no reason other than to see the guy fail, which he did. Richard had aced Remedies but was now having problems with Remorse, a course that was infinitely harder and had no final, just a lot of labs. He turned his thoughts to Laura—what else was there?—wondering what had attracted him so much that he had devoted an entire journal to her. Was it her red hair, her lithe body, those hazel eyes that sparkled like mica? It was all coming back now, although what he remembered was the *memory* of her hair, legs, eyes, that smile as natural and exotic as smoke. In reality, it could have been any one of those things or none of them. Even so, she had been his friend and lover at a time in his life when those things mattered most. Strange to admit, but they mattered even more now.

"Laura."

He wasn't used to the name and had to sound out the syllables, repeating them again and again in the heat. Sometimes he lengthened the first syllable, sometimes the last, sometimes both, but each time he got a rush he hadn't felt in years. And then, suddenly, he was back there, far from Ambergris Caye and the tinny-accented English of these polite and shiny but altogether ludicrous people who neither knew him nor the hell he had been through. He was a dude again, breathing in the thick, semen-scented air of summer, skirting the hot exhaust of buses, wiping the layer of grime that Center City had deposited on his skin, watching her move with what he discovered later on was grace. He hadn't known what that was until he saw with his own eyes how virtue and poise could come together in a pair of lightly perspiring, slightly parted teenage thighs. They had made him tremble.

"*Lawe—raah.*"

Had it really been that long ago? As he thought about it, he realized how many years, how many experiences, people, and places he had been through as if they had all been pairs of shoes thrown thoughtlessly into a closet. Was Laura another pair of shoes? If so, she would have to be sandals. But that couldn't be. She was different: demanding and tough, to be sure, but authentic. He loved the fact that he never really knew where he stood with her, never certain if she was his or not, which was a big part of the attraction. She was clever that way and such a tease that for a time he thought about kidnapping her, even hatching a fantastic plot with a stolen car and an escape route to Wyoming, where they would settle down like husband and wife in a lookout post in a forest. He was less clever than her but duplicitous to the core, which was also genetic and something that had been refined through rigorous legal training. We must have been the perfect pair, he thought, realizing almost instantly that he had failed at that, too. And why not? He had failed at everything that counted in life—love, marriage, family, friendship, career, money, traveling, you name it. Funny, but the one thing he was perfect at—batting a thousand—was failure. At that, he had a bust in Cooperstown.

He had to get out of Belize. That much was certain. This back-water town was never part of the plan but just one of those things that happened along the way, one screw-up followed by another and another until he found himself at the edge of the world instead of on top of it. Back in Philadelphia, they had reminded him bluntly that it was his responsibility as head of Mergers & Acquisitions not only to go on this trip but to come back with the necessary valuations and analyses for the client. Simple enough, except when it wasn't. Funny how responsibility turned into despair and despair into surrender. He had been set up by his best friend and coworker from the firm. He never saw it coming, maybe couldn't have seen it, not even as a member of a severely paranoid family that his therapist had once said could be the subject of "an entire psychiatric conference." As far as he knew, he had always been that way, expecting disaster to announce itself with the next phone call or knock at the door. That was just his style, his standard operating procedure. Still, he wasn't always like that. When he was younger he had hopes and dreams like everyone else. He also had this irrepressible drive to find out what lay around the corner, convinced that he could do anything, go anywhere, and knock anyone down who stood in his way, not realizing that *he* was the one who stood in the way. Then, true to his nature, when he finally figured it out, he couldn't stop in time and proceeded to knock himself down.

So, he decided to read the journal after all. He didn't have much else to do, and the prosecutor wasn't supposed to be back till Monday, if at all. If Richard had learned anything during his time in jail, apart from a little Garífuna and how to tell when a mango is ripe (it should feel like a young woman's breast when pressed—you could also sniff them, and how exciting would that be?), it was that dates and appointments were not what you would call an exact science down here. Hell, science wasn't an exact science. Besides, everything seemed to have led up to this one moment, this one chance to go back in time so that he could, if not exactly make things right, at least relive them with the heart and mind of an adult. He might even forgive himself, as impossible as that sounded. It would be something to tell his therapist about if he ever got back home.

He opened to the first page, hoping it wouldn't be too painful, but, then again, considering what was in it and how old he was at the time, how could it not be? He recognized the writing right away. It was jerky and brash, the spacing was uneven, and the words ran together like schoolboys goofing off in line. God, how many times had he done that? He remembered the day a kid named Jimmy Mott kept bumping into him from behind until he finally turned around and shoved him. Naturally, Mott fell back into Ann Miller, who was wearing a pleated dress with patent leather shoes like Jane in the *Dick and Jane* reader. She fell and cut her knee, and Richard was hauled off to the principal's office, which was the first time he had to do time. He was scolded by Mr. Farnese and had to write an apology to both Jimmy and Ann, which he had objected to so strongly that the principal called his mother in, who was so upset by her son's "criminal" behavior that she had completely forgotten what little English she knew.

Some of the journal entries were brief, others more detailed. Most of it, though, was highly stylized, especially for a fifteen-year-old. Had he been that precocious, or was he just a smart-ass? His mother had given him the journal as a present for his birthday, since he had been accepted as a reporter on the school newspaper at St. Rita of Cascia High School (SRCHS)—*Veritas, Unitas, Caritas!* St. Rita being famous, of course, as the patron saint of the impossible who "suffered the wounds of love." He remembered how he had written everything down, from random dialogue to full conversations, reflections, and opinions about the day's events, often making it up and embellishing the rest. It was a kind of fictional diary or handwritten blog, including drawings in the margins, running commentary, and footnotes. You had to have footnotes; it wasn't official without proper notes and citations. He remembered, too, how it had ended with the unimaginable, an event that had truly wounded him, leading to an adult life marked by cynicism and doubt, as if being a Mercurius weren't enough. In the end, it wasn't.

The Top Secret Journal of Richard P.[1] Mercurius
(Hands off!)

Friday, June 18, 1976

The radio comes on early in our house. No matter what, it's always in the background like traffic or dogs barking or jets flying overhead. Every morning mom listens to WIBG, "The Big 99," while she makes breakfast for me and Kornél. This morning they said it would be another hot one, in the nineties, and if it hit 99 they would give away ninety-nine free tickets for Father's Day during the Phillies' homestand against the Reds. You'd get to see Steve Carlton and Mike Schmidt play against Pete Rose and the Big Red Machine for free. So I wrote the number down while I got ready for the meeting. Mr. Andrade told me to get there on time, cause even though I have a "way with words" and am "really smart" (he said that), I'm always late and sooner or later it will come back to bite me in the ass. He said that, too. I knew it would be close, cause I left the house late after waiting for Kornél, who was in the bathroom forever, doing whatever. I don't even want to know. I hate being late. I also hate showing up for a meeting all out of breath and sweating, but that's exactly what happened. I caught a late bus and had to race down Washington to get to school. They promised

---

1 *Don't ask. It's Hungarian. I also don't know how secret this will be, but I'll do my best.*

me the lead article for the fall issue of *The Review*, and I was really pumped about it. I was going to interview the new vice principal, a guy who had spent time in prison for embezzlement of funds at Central Penn Bank. Now he was leading high school kids. You couldn't make up a better story. Well, I could, but then it would be all made up.

And then it happened.

"Merk, we need you to cover the football camp in August," Glenn, the editor-in-chief and a senior, said as I burst through the door of Mr. Andrade's office.

Glenn had thick glasses and weighed about two hundred pounds. He had scored near perfect on the SATs and had early acceptance at Penn, Haverford, Swarthmore, and Ursinus, which meant that he had no trouble throwing his weight around.

"*What?*"

"Page one is off, football and the sports page are on."

"But you said I could do the interview!"

"Change of plans. We just found out Scot's family is moving to Arizona over the summer and there's nobody else who can do it. You'll be fine, don't worry. By the way, this is Laura. She's agreed to do the interview for you."

"*For me?*"

"That's right."

"Hi, I'm Laura Fedora," a redheaded girl in jeans and an Aerosmith t-shirt said, smiling. She sat on the floor against the wall with one leg crossed over a raised knee, her sandaled foot pumping back and forth. She put her hand out but I didn't take it.

"*Laura Fedora?* You're kidding, right?"

"No, not at all," she said. "And you are?"

"Richard."

"Does Richard have a last name?"

"Mercurius."

"*Mercurius?* You're kidding, right?"

"No, it's Hungarian."

"It doesn't sound Hungarian."

"Well, it is."

"You mean like goulash?"

"That's not funny."

"Sure it is," she said, winking at me.

Then Mr. Andrade said, "Look, if you two want to flirt, do it on your own time. We've got work to do."

"But we weren't flirting!"

"Oh? What do you call it, then?"

I shifted my weight back and forth, not sure what to say, and then everybody laughed, including Laura Fedora, which I didn't get at all.

So I watched this girl with a hat for a name for the rest of the meeting, and I could tell she was watching me back, waiting for me to say something smart, which I thought about doing but didn't because, to tell you the truth, even though I was pissed (I still don't believe it!), she was amazing. Her hair was this strange orange color like a bowl of yams at Thanksgiving, and when she smiled I thought it was the sexiest smile I'd ever seen in my entire life. But as terrific as all that was, what got me were her feet, which were so clean she could have just gotten a pedicure. Maybe she did and maybe she didn't—I don't know about those things—but when I tell you they were perfect I mean PERFECT, like feet you'd see in a magazine or on TV. Her toenails were pink and didn't have a nick on them. I checked. *This little piggy went to market, this little piggy stayed home, this little piggy had roast beef, this little piggy had none.* Through the entire meeting I couldn't take my eyes off them, even when Glenn was talking about the sports page and how I had to make room for the team picture and don't forget the soccer team with that new kid who moved here from Brazil whose father was a janitor at the school.

"You probably know him, Merk, he's a striker. The kid, not the father. What's his name?"

"Huh?" I said, looking up.

"His name, the kid's name."

"I dunno."

"Well, find out."

"Right."

Glenn paused, staring at me through his grimy glasses like some early-acceptance goldfish.

"Hey, are you all right?"

"Oh, sure," I said, which somehow got everybody laughing again.

Maybe they knew something I didn't, like what happened to me was what Mrs. Dudoit in French 202 calls a *coup de foudre,* a lightning bolt that strikes people in love. Or was it *coup d'état?* Whatever it was, I decided that this Sunday I would go to her parish, which I found out from Brenda Conti is Maria Goretti, and get my assignment back. I'm not going to let her steal my article like that, no matter what Glenn says or how much I think about her feet, which is pretty much every minute of every hour of every day.

Sunday, June 20
Father's Day

This morning the temperature dropped fifteen degrees and we never hit 99, so whoever thought of the stunt saved a bunch of money and got extra publicity for the radio station, WIBBAGE, on Father's Day. I was on the bus by 9:30, headed for Maria Goretti, hoping to run into Laura. At first, I thought I was out of luck, but then I saw her slip out a side door before Mass ended. It took me a while to recognize her, because she wasn't in jeans and a t-shirt anymore. She wore a yellow sundress with blue dots and a blue sash and a straw hat with a blue ribbon. I don't think I've ever seen anybody that beautiful before. I stood there staring at her, and it was like watching a rainbow against the gray walls of the church and the grotto with a statue of Maria Goretti that was filled with dirty plastic flowers in dirty Ball jars. For a second I couldn't breathe. I had to remind myself. *Coup d'état,* take two.

"Richard, what are you doing here?" she said, recognizing me right away and skipping down the steps.

"What? Oh, nothing."

"What do you mean nothing?"

"You know, nothing."

She looked me over and said, "Do you live around here?"

"Nope."

"Do you go to church here?"

"No."

"So what are you doing here?"

I couldn't answer.

"You didn't come here to see me, did you?"

I nodded.

"About what?"

This was too much to take, so I cleared my throat and did what I always do in situations like these.

"Well, I came here to apologize for the way I treated you at school the other day. It was awful."

"What?"

"I came here to apologize—"

"No, I heard that. I mean really?"

I shrugged and looked up at Maria Goretti. "May God strike me dead."

She paused for a second, but instead of telling me what a crock of horse manure that was, said, "I think that's very sweet."

"You do?"

"Of course."

Then she said, "Tell you what, I'm going to the park to meet my brother and nonno. Want to come along?"

"What's a nonno?"

"My grandpa. Want to come?"

"Sure."

And just like that, in the wink of an eye, we were walking down the street like a couple, our hands so close they almost touched. I swear a couple of times they almost did. I couldn't believe it. We crossed over to Garibaldi Park, which had sycamore trees and benches and a bandstand with a white, wooden railing and a green roof. She introduced me to her grandpa, this ancient guy, thin, wearing a woolen sweater under his jacket and a beat-up hat, a fedora, which I thought was pretty funny. He was with someone who must have been Laura's brother.

"Piacere," nonno said, getting up from a bench to greet me. His eyes were light blue and watery and he had gray stubble. Then he tipped his hat and a bunch of grapefruit peels fell to the ground. He had sneaked out of church during the homily and gone to the park, where he sat eating grapefruit and smoking cigarettes with Laura's brother.

"Who's the geek?" her brother asked.

"His name is Richard and he's not a geek."

"If you say so. Friend of yours?"

"We work on the school newspaper," I told him.

He grunted and said, "Really?"

I looked over at Laura, who said, "His name is Enzo, short for Lorenzo. But everybody just calls him Enz."

"I like that, a nickname for a nickname."

He looked away, kind of annoyed, but then handed me a Marlboro, which I took (I've smoked cigarettes before with Tommy Lindeman). We sat there smoking while Laura walked nonno around the park. Enz had a smooth face like a baby with high cheekbones and a straight nose, a guy version of Laura except for his dark eyes. He kept talking about some problem he was having with an oil leak in his car, a '63 Corvair convertible, but I couldn't take my eyes off Laura—her arms, her neck, the blue sash, the way her body moved underneath the dress. I could see her legs through the dress as the sun shone through it when she walked on the other side of the park.

I had one cigarette, then another, and by the time I finished the second I heard Enz say, "Can you believe that?"

"No, it's unbelievable, really."

"Got that right," he said, flicking a cigarette butt onto the grass. "I mean, what am I, an idiot or something?"

"Nope."

"Damn straight."

"So, what will you do?" I asked.

"Forget him, that's what. I'll replace the pushrod myself."

"Way to go."

"Yep."

He stood up to leave but then went on some more about idiots and pushrods. I tried to listen but was watching Laura the whole time. At last, Laura came back with nonno, who pulled a dirty handkerchief out of his pocket and kept hacking into it till I thought he would vomit.

"Time to go," she announced.

"Already?"

"I have to get nonno back."

"But I thought we could talk."

"About what?"

"You know, about the paper."

She looked over at Enz, who turned and started walking away.

"All right. Come by tomorrow."

"Where?"

"Here. I'll meet you here at eleven o'clock."

"Okay."

"Ciao," nonno said, turning around, waving.

"Ciao," I said, waving back.

I don't know if he heard me, but the three of them left the park headed east toward the river, Laura and her brother on either side of nonno. I was so excited I sat there for a half hour before heading home. I felt like I had died and was sitting in a park in the middle of heaven. I could have sat there forever and eventually God would come along in a green Parks & Rec uniform to empty the trash cans.

Later, when I got home I gave dad a card and the Stargazer Astronomer's Wheel I had ordered through the mail. It came in enough time and I had hidden it on the shelf in my closet with my baseball card collection. He said he liked it. We looked up the date and checked the constellations. It was pretty cool. Even mom said so, and she doesn't know anything about astronomy.

Monday, June 21
The Family Fedora

This morning I went back to Garibaldi Park. I made sure I got there early (it was easy, because I didn't sleep at all last night) and sat on the same bench, waiting for Laura Fedora. I spotted her right away. This time, she had her hair pulled back in a black headband, and she wore a sweatshirt and black tights. I think they were tights. When she got close enough we said hi, and then she plopped down on the bench next to me.

"Nice day," I said like a major idiot.

She nodded. I waited and then said, "So, how's nonno?"

"He's fine. I left him listening to opera."

"Opera?"

"Yeah, that's one of his hobbies."

"Wow, I don't know anybody who does that."

"Well, he does. He knows a lot about it, too, but you can't ask him anything, cause he doesn't have much patience with people. If you ever talk to him, make sure you have a favorite opera, a favorite tenor, and a favorite recording. Otherwise, he'll throw something at you."

"Really?"

"He does it all the time. This morning he threw a piece of toast at my mother, and she chased him around the kitchen table."

"She doesn't have a favorite opera?"

"No, silly, she burnt his toast."

"Oh."

I couldn't be sure if she was pulling my leg, so I didn't say anything. One thing I could be sure of, though, was that this girl sitting next to me was absolutely beautiful. Her eyes were so clear I could practically see through them, like you could see the sky in them (no lie), and she had the sexiest lips I've ever seen, curved and full but not too puffy or pouty like stuck-up girls. I don't like stuck-up girls or their lips. And I don't like puffy on lips or anything else except Cheese Puffs. I really like Cheese Puffs. Looking at her lips and how they flared at the corners of her mouth got me thinking about her mouth and other things, but you have to keep your eye on the ball. At least that's what Mr. Ryan, my homeroom teacher and the baseball coach, says and he ought to know. Keep your eye on the ball.

"So, what did you want to talk about?" Laura said.

"What?"

"You said you wanted to talk about *The Review*."

I was ready for this, because I spent the whole morning rehearsing. I even practiced on the bus, which made an old black woman with groceries in a wire cart move up toward the driver. Corn husks were sticking out of the top of her bag and she kept staring over them like I was a maniac or something.

"Well, I wondered if you'd want to team up with me on some stories for the paper, maybe even write a column together."

"It's funny you should say that, cause Brenda and I are working on a story together. Mister Andrade already approved it."

"Oh. So what is it?"

"You know who Christine Chubbuck was, right?"

"Sure."

"Well, it's about the pressure she was under as a female television reporter in a male dominated industry and how it caused her to shoot herself on live TV. She's one of my heroines, an inspiration to women everywhere, which is why I want to study broadcast journalism in college and follow in her footsteps."

"She shot herself?"

"On television."

"And she's an inspiration?"

"She gave her life."

I stared at her. This was even worse than the toast story. I sort of remembered that happening but not really. I think it was in Florida or somewhere with palm trees. I can't imagine being inspired by somebody who shoots herself in front of television cameras, especially in a place with beaches and a whole lot of orange juice. Who does that?

"I guess that's that," I said.

"Maybe not. We could do something else sometime."

"You mean it?"

"Why not?" Then, almost whispering, she leaned over and said, "Brenda told me about you, you know."

"Told you?"

"How you asked her all kinds of questions about me. She said you were very pushy."

"She said that, *pushy*?"

"No, the word she used was *nosy*."

"Hey, I'm not pushy or nosy. I was just trying to find you, that's all."

"To talk about the paper?"

"Yeah."

"I dunno."

"What do you mean?"

"Seems like an awful lot of trouble just to talk about a story. Are you sure there wasn't something else?"

"No, that was it, honest. As a reporter, I take my journalism very seriously. You should know that about me."

I didn't mean it to be funny or bragging or anything like that, but it got her laughing so hard she arched her head back and showed her teeth, which were straight and perfect like her feet, which meant that her family had enough money to buy her braces. As she laughed, I looked down at her white tennis shoes, which she wore without socks. Even her ankles, curved and delicate, were the sexiest things I'd ever seen.

"That's pretty funny, Richard. Is that what I should call you, 'Richard?'"

"If you want."

"Does anybody else call you Richard?"

"At home they do."

"What about at school?"

"Well, the guys on the track team—I'm on the track team, you know—"

"Yeah, I heard. You're a sprinter and they call you Merk. You even have little wings painted on your locker."

"How did you know that?"

"Brenda told me. She knows everything and everyone. That's why she's on the Yearbook Committee."

She flicked her hair back, adjusted the headband, and blew a bubble that covered half her face. I swear I didn't know she had gum in her mouth.

"But I'm still doing the interview," she said after snapping the bubble, which was so loud a woman with a stroller turned around.

"Sure."

"You didn't come here to ask for your assignment back?"

"God no," I told her. "I just wanted to talk to you about working together, but it sounds like you're too busy."

I didn't know what else to say and stuffed my hands into my pockets, hoping she wouldn't ask any more questions.

"Well, maybe we could write a sports column together," she said. "Not right now but later. I've been thinking about playing tennis, anyway. I've got a cousin who plays and he said he'd teach me. He's ranked, you know."

"That's great."

I didn't get what tennis had to do with flying toast and suicide, but as far as I was concerned it was just ping-pong with a bunch of grunting and squeaking. I remembered all the hype about Billie Jean King and the match on TV—mom watched it—but for the most part tennis was for people who pulled up to the front of fancy restaurants and threw their keys at the valet. You had to have plenty of dough and time. We had plenty of neither, but Laura's family must have had both. They could afford braces, college, and tennis lessons with some hot-shot cousin. I didn't even own a racket. Well, I did, but it was a wooden one left in the basement by the people who lived in the house before us, some Main Line types who also left a strongbox filled with S&H Green stamps (mom was beside herself). The owner had his name and the name of his team stenciled on the handle: Clyde Bowden, Lions Club. I guess it could have been where he played, I don't know. Who names their kid Clyde, anyway?

"I have to go now," Laura said.

"But you just got here."

"I know, but I have to help with lunch. I just came to find out what you wanted and now I know, so I'd better get going."

She started to leave, cutting across the grass, and I felt my chest tighten. Then she turned around real quick and said, "Hey, are you hungry?" It took me a while to answer, cause even the way she turned was something else: a pivot in the grass on the ball of her foot and a toss of her head, the headband framing her face, hands on her hips. It was like ballet with an attitude. I swear I've never seen anything like it. Like a swan or something, with bubble gum.

"Sure."

"Then have lunch with us."

"Really?"

"Why not?"

"Well, I—"

"Come on!"

So we walked back to her house, which was off Wharton not far from the park. She lived at 305 South Adriana, a three-story row home with aluminum siding and a bay window. Inside, the window was covered with thick gold and white curtains, but I could see a blue Virgin Mary on a marble stand and a fancy lamp with a porcelain base. Flowerpots lined the front of the house along with a wooden bench and chairs, and there was a cherry tree in a patch of earth by the curb. Air conditioners stuck out of the upper windows, leaving little puddles on the sidewalk below, and, like our house, there was an American flag on the porch. I followed her inside past the screen door with an enormous metal "F" and waited in the hall while she went into the kitchen to talk to her mother. She was gone forever, so I went to the staircase where I heard music coming from the basement, which must have been nonno's room. It sounded like opera but not the STP commercial kind, more like Looney Tunes. From that angle, I could see into the kitchen and Laura's mother standing at the stove. She was a small woman with dark hair and a really white face. Then they came out to the hall, Laura behind her mother, who wore a flowered housedress and face cream that some women put on to look beautiful. Her hair was in pink rollers and she held a spatula with a burnt pepper stuck on the end. Her other hand was on her hip. She looked like a Zulu warrior I had seen in *Encyclopedia Britannica* in the school library.

"So, you're Richard?"

"Yes, ma'am," I said, stepping back.

"Richard what?"

"Mercurius," Laura answered from behind.

"Like the car?"

"No, mom, it's Mer-'kur-ee-us.'"

"Oh—and what does he want?"

"He doesn't want anything. I invited him over."

"You mean now? I didn't think you meant now."

"I meant now."

Mrs. Fedora leaned forward, squinting, spatula in hand, and said, "All right, come in and have lunch with us, but no funny stuff, I'm telling you."

She had eyes like a deer, nearly black, and sharp eyebrows like Laura's, which made me think they got them done at the same place. I followed them into the kitchen, and I wanted to tell her I had no intention of doing anything funny but decided to shut up.

"You can sit there next to Laura," Mrs. Fedora said, pointing to a chair at the end of the table.

It was one of those polished wooden chairs with a seat so big and thick you can slide around in it. A radio with a gold dial was playing next to the stove, which was splattered with grease.

"So, Richard..."

"Yes, ma'am."

"What do you do?"

"Do?"

"—Mom, he doesn't do anything. He's a student at Saint Rita's."

"Right, I forgot....Oh, *you're* the Hungarian kid from the newspaper. Laura told me all about you and the goulash thing."

"Yes, ma'am. I'm on the school newspaper with Laura. We're going to write a story together."

"You are? About what?"

"I don't know."

"You're writing a story and you don't know about what?"

"We haven't decided yet."

"I'm still working with Brenda," Laura said, "but after that we might do a sports column together."

"Sports? My God, Laura, everybody does sports these days. It's ridiculous. It's boring. What about the queen's visit? You know, she's coming here next month for the Bicentennial. The Queen of England coming to Philly! Why don't you write about that?"

Mrs. Fedora turned toward me, expecting an answer, but, honest to God, I didn't know what to say. I had never thought about the queen but wondered how we could write an article about a woman whose great-great grandfather or somebody like that had burned down the White House. Then, just as I was about to say something stupid, nonno came in. He talked in a raspy voice and held up two fingers. Mrs. Fedora yelled at him in Italian, which made him stand still, blink, and then walk away.

"Richard, do you like peppers and eggs?"

"Yes, ma'am."

"All right, then, Laura, come over here and finish this. And what's all this 'yes ma'am' and 'no ma'am' business? What, are we in the South? It makes me feel old!"

She cackled, threw up her hands, and disappeared into a bathroom just off the kitchen, slamming the door behind her.

"Well, now you've met my mother," Laura said. "She's a little hyper."

"She's nice."

"Just wait till she starts in about the queen. She won't let it go. Once she gets fixed on something, she doesn't give up."

"Must run in the family," I said.

It was supposed to be funny, but Laura just smirked and scraped peppers and eggs into a big, green bowl. So I sat back and looked around the kitchen. Writers have to be good observers, so I make it a point to notice as much around me as possible. I don't do it all the time, sometimes I forget. Anyway, there were pictures of Jesus, the pope, and Mayor Rizzo on the walls. A large wooden fork and spoon hung, crucified, on the wall behind me. There was a clock carved out of a piece of redwood that said, "Big Basin, California." The refrigerator looked like ours except bigger and green like an avocado, and the stove, also avocado, was electric with coils on top. A burned espresso pot sat on a back coil. Past the bathroom, a hallway led to a back room that had an ironing board with a pink basket of laundry on top. Magazines and books were stacked on the floor. Past that was a window looking out to the yard, and I could see a fig tree with its branches held up by wooden poles next to a garage with a broken window and sagging roof.

Then I looked back at Laura and realized that we were alone and this was the perfect time for me to check her out, so that's just what I did. Most of the time, like when I'm in class and I see a nice-looking girl, could be in the hallway or the next row, I pretend that I have the power to go so fast that, compared to everybody else, time stands still. They're moving at normal speed, but it's like they're frozen and I can do whatever I want cause I'm moving so fast that they can't even see me. I imagine doing the same thing on a basketball court. Got the idea from a *Star Trek* episode. That's what it was like now, *Star Trek*.

I started at her waist, where I could see the black tights underneath her sweatshirt, and went down to her behind, which was round like a delicious plum, but I couldn't see her dimples or the curved line separating her cheeks. I followed the tights as they dipped toward her thighs and legs, which were sleek like a gazelle's, a slice of avocado from the oven peering out between them. Oh, to be an avocado! And then—was it really that hot in here?—to her heels, which were naked and smooth and slender. I did this not once or twice but three times! It was awesome, even though, I have to admit, I've never even seen a gazelle except on *Wild Kingdom*, and then it was being ripped apart by hyenas. I must have moaned out loud or something, because Laura turned around, smiling. I smiled back. Then, looking past me toward the kitchen door, she yelled, "Hi, daddy! I didn't see you standing there. Were you there long?"

"LONG ENOUGH!" a voice boomed behind me. It actually vibrated through me. "And who is this?"

I shot up, but the chair was so heavy it pressed into the back of my knees and I collapsed onto the seat again.

"Here, let me help you with that. It's kinda tricky," Enz said, smirking, pulling the chair out for me.

"Daddy, this is Richard, a friend of mine from school. He's having lunch with us," Laura said, coming up to both of us and kissing her father. "Richard, this is my father."

"Hello, Mister Fedora," I stuttered, holding out my hand, which was my second mistake. My first, I guess, was being born. He looked down like he had never seen a hand before, took it in his, and crushed it.

"Daddy"—Alberto Angelo Santorella Fedora—was five-and-a-half feet tall with red bushy hair, red bushy eyebrows, and a red bushy face. He owned and ran a used car dealership on South Street named Fedora Auto Sales and Transport (his business cards said

FAST! and had a little guy in a tuxedo and fedora racing across the bottom just like Monopoly Man). Laura told me later he made all the salesmen wear fedoras, but if you worked there long enough he'd reimburse you for the fedora and even buy you a new one (beaver). He was a tree trunk of a man with a thick neck and forearms and ears that stuck out. He glared at me, and I saw that his eyes were light like Laura's, except one had a red half-moon, which made him look like a werewolf.[2] I was starting to think I wouldn't make it out alive.

"So, does Richard have a last name?" he asked without taking his eyes off me. I thought I saw red flames coming out of his nose.

"Mercurius," Laura said.

"What?"

"Mercurius," she repeated.

"You mean like the car?"

"No, Mer-'kur-ee-us."

"Richard Mercurius?"

"Yes."

"What's that, Greek?"

"Hungarian."

"It doesn't sound Hungarian."

"It's as Hungarian as goulash," Laura said.

Mr. Fedora grunted and then said to me, "Kid, forget goulash. With a name like that you could open a burger joint!"

Everybody burst out laughing and I did, too, even though I didn't think it was funny, not coming from a guy named after a hat, but what could I say? They had home court advantage. In fact, the only one I could count on was nonno, and they had locked him away in the basement. So, I went along with the joke.

---

2 *See my drawing of "Tree Man," half oak, half werewolf. It's pretty good, I think. I like drawing. First, I do a sketch and then I fill it in with colored pencils or a marker.*

"Sit down, son," Mr. Fedora said, getting serious. "No, not there, *there.*"

He pointed to a chair on the opposite side of the table, so that now my back was to the stove. In case there was any doubt as to why, he added, "I don't want you getting distracted from our little talk."

"Sir?"

"Just a couple of questions."

"*Dad,*" Laura moaned.

"What? I just want to know who I'm having lunch with."

"But I told you already. He's a friend of mine from school and we work on the newspaper together."

"Sure, all right, honey." Then, turning toward me, "You're the one from the park?"

"Yes, sir."

"They told me about you. My father said you were at Mass."

"Your father?"

"Nonno," Laura said.

"Oh, right. I was at Maria Goretti."

"But the Mass is in Italian. Laura, isn't the Mass in Italian? Isn't that the one you went to yesterday?"

She tried to answer but he cut her off. "So, tell me, Richard, why go to an Italian Mass if you're not Italian and don't speak it? I'm guessing you don't speak it, right?"

I nodded.

"So, explain it to me."

"Explain?"

"Explain."

I didn't like where this was headed, but I couldn't admit that the only reason I was there was to see Laura, so I relied on one of the few things I know for sure.

"Well, see, I take Latin and it's not that far off."

"Say again?"

"I take Latin and it—"

"No, I heard you. What does that mean?"

"I'm in Latin at school and Latin is a lot like Italian, at least it's closer than French. I'm in French class, too, cause I want to read French literature and poetry and things like that when I go to college. But Latin is closer to Italian than French is. So it was easier to follow the Mass, linguistically, I mean."

He sat back and stared at me. Enz coughed and looked around the room, still smirking. Laura stood at the stove with her mouth open. I guess it hadn't gone very well. I thought about sliding under the table.

"Al, leave the kid alone," Mrs. Fedora said, coming out of the bathroom and adjusting the straps of her dress. She had rinsed the cream from her face and taken the rollers out of her hair. I never thought I'd be so happy to see her.

"He's not Italian, he was in the park, he goes to school with Laura, and he's Catholic. What more do you want to know?"

"You're Catholic?"

"Yes, sir."

"Parents?"

"Two."

"Catholic?"

"Yes, but my father isn't very religious. I mean, he is in his own way, which is a little different. My mother goes to Mass every Sunday and sings in the choir. She practically lives at church."

"See, Al? Did he pass the test?" Mrs. Fedora asked. "All right, let's eat. Enzo, call your grandfather up here and tell him súbito."

"Yes, ma'am," Enz said. "I'll do it linguistically."

"Very funny. That's really very funny. You should win an award, you know." Then, turning toward me she said, "I'm living in a house of comedians. Remember that, Robert. They're all comedians here."

"Richard," Laura said.

After Enz came back with nonno, things calmed down except for Mrs. Fedora insisting that I write an article about the queen's visit (I had to include a paragraph about her hats, because people would want to know that sort of thing) and Enz going on about his car that leaked oil, water, and gas.

"What it leaks is money," Mr. Fedora said. "I told you to put it up for sale. I'll make sure it gets a good price."

"I can't, dad, it's a classic."

"Classic, my ass."

"Al, watch your language," Mrs. Fedora said.

Al grunted, looked in my direction, and took up the attack again. "It's a piece of junk."

"How can you say that? The car is a classic. Everybody knows that."

"Is that right?"

"That's right."

"Well, let's see. Richard, is the sixty-three Corvair a classic or not?"

"Convertible," Enz added.

"Convertible."

They both stared at me, I choked, Mrs. Fedora whacked me on the back a couple of times, and up came a piece of green pepper. They didn't miss a beat and started arguing about what constitutes a classic—age, styling, popularity, or awards. I could have gone with any of them, but no one asked my opinion after that. For some reason, nonno kept scraping eggs onto my plate. I thought he might throw something, but he kept an eye on Mrs. Fedora and more or less behaved himself. When they finished yelling, they started calling me "Dick Mercury" till Laura shouted something in Italian, which led to a long pause and then more yelling. But the meal was okay—at least up to the choking part—and we had espresso and peaches with Cool Whip for dessert, which I liked. I noticed that nonno drank his wine with peach slices in his glass. A lot of them. I noticed, too, Laura noticing me noticing her, which made it a great day, even after Enz drove me home in his classic—bright yellow like a canary—and it broke down at Market. It didn't matter, though, cause I had just had lunch with an angel.

Tuesday, June 22

Mom said it's "high time" for me to get a summer job to help with the expenses around the house and my tuition, which will be due in August even though school just let out.[3] So I took Tommy Lindeman's advice and talked to Mr. Andrade about being a counselor at the St. Rita Day Camp. Mr. Andrade is the director, which he does to earn extra money in addition to being the faculty advisor to *The Review*, since his wife is expecting their second kid and they need a bigger place. They rent a house in the neighborhood with one bedroom next to a tattoo parlor called the "Dog Tag Tattoo," which he says isn't the right environment for his family. They had an opening and he hired me for $3.00 an hour, which is pretty good considering all I have to do is watch kids play kickball and make sure they don't get hurt, which I can do no problem. Lindeman is the lifeguard, so he gets $4.50 an hour, cause if they drown or crack their heads open from running around, St. Rita's is in big trouble. Lindeman has the cool job, but I don't mind. It's his neck.

Apart from making money and having something to do this summer, I'll be close enough to South Adriana to walk over to Laura's at lunchtime or after work. I don't know what to do about her father, though. He doesn't like me and thinks I'm only after one thing. He's right about that, but from what I've seen, Big Al hasn't got anything to worry about. In fact, *I'm* the one who should worry. Laura's smarter than me and savvy about everything, or at

---

3 Is "high time" like high tide? Is there a "low time?" I said that to her, but she just gave me the look. I don't know where mom gets this stuff, except maybe TV.

least pretty sure of herself, which is worse. That whole thing with the television reporter spooked me, because other than studying French, which Mrs. Dudoit says I'm good at (*très bon, Richard*), I've got nothing to offer her as cool as broadcast journalism or anything like that. And I bet she's only interested in upper classmen. I'd ask Brenda about it, but the blabbermouth would probably snitch on me the first chance she got. I know she would. She'd deny it, too. Brenda Conti has a Big Mouth and an even BIGGER BUTT. I'm drawing a picture of it in the margin, with zits.

Tuesday, June 29
Figgy Love

I've got a problem. After one week of work, it's not what I thought it would be, which happens to me all the time. I should probably sit down and figure it out, cause things never turn out the way I expect them to. It's the story of my life. They put me in charge of the equipment room, which means all the balls, bats, rackets, nets, gloves, floats, and shuttlecocks. Yes, shuttlecocks. I also have to keep track of the board games like checkers and backgammon so that none of the pieces gets lost. There are about a million pieces. Then there's "Animal Habitat." Some genius had the bright idea of turning one of the props from last year's musical, *Oklahoma!*, into a pen for farm animals like chickens, rabbits, hamsters, and these

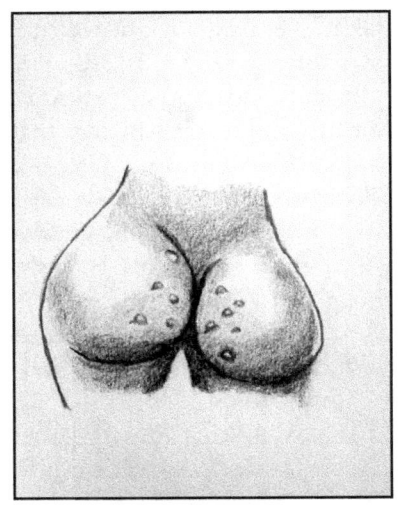

two little pigs that are as annoying as hell. I swear, all they do is run around and squeal. Mr. Andrade says they're very smart, but smart or not I don't want to go near them, let alone pick up their shit, which is part of the job. I never knew this about pig shit, but it's a lot like baby shit, smells like it, too, and smears like warm peanut butter (chunky). And that's not even the worst part. The worst part of the job is not having enough time for Laura. I haven't seen her all week and forgot to ask for her phone number, so I'll have to get it from Brenda-Big-Butt. I don't want to do that, cause I'll look like a geek, but what else can I do? Then again, Laura hasn't tried to get in touch with me, either, so I don't know where this is going except nowhere *FAST!*

The weekend was a killer and by Monday morning I was climbing the walls, so I went to the portables next to the gym to talk to Mr. Andrade. He was at his desk, reading the *Inquirer* sports page and listening to the Big 99. He wore a red and white St. Rita polo shirt and shorts. He also had the hairiest legs I've ever seen. I don't think I'll ever have legs that hairy.

"Well, if it isn't Mercurio," he said, looking up and smiling. "So, tell me, what's the new news at the new court?"

He's always pulling crap like that, either to be funny or trick you. I guess that's what English teachers do. I was ready for him, though.

"There's no new news at the new court, sir, but the old news."

"Excellent, Mercurio. Where's it from?"

"As You Like It."

"Well, what do you know? Somebody's paying attention in class. Nice work. So, what can I do you for?"

I cleared my throat. "I have this problem."

"Squiggly and Piggly?"

"No, not exactly."

"The kid with the bloody nose?"

"No, he's fine. It's something else."

"Really?" he said, turning down the radio. "What is it?"

"I need to leave early today."

"How early?"

"Right now."

"Any particular reason?"

"It's personal."

"Personal?" he repeated.

"I mean it's not about work or school or anything like that."

"I see."

"It's sort of—"

"Personal."

"Exactly."

There was this long pause like he expected me to tell him what was so personal that I couldn't tell him, but the whole point was that it was personal so how could I? I should have known. Anytime you say something's personal it gets everybody's attention. It's like whispering. If you don't want people to hear what you're saying, don't whisper. Say it out loud. Nobody'll pay any attention then, because they're always talking instead of listening. That's what people do—talk and gab, gab and talk. Nobody ever listens.

"You in some sort of trouble?"

"Oh no, nothing like that, it's just that I have something to do that can't wait."

"Can't wait?"

"No, sir."

He looked at me like he knew damn well that something was up, but there was no way I was going to tell him what was going on between me and Laura. Or not going on. It would have been too embarrassing.

"All right, you can leave," he said.

I was all ready to thank him and back out the door when he said point blank, "It's the Fedora girl, isn't it?"

I froze.

"Sure it is," he said, smiling.

"How did you know?"

"Because you've been acting strange ever since our last meeting. Besides, she came by here on Friday looking for you."

"*What?*"

"She was here with Brenda Conti. They were working on their article and stopped by to see you. I told them you were in the Habitat cleaning up."

"But they never came by!"

He shrugged. I couldn't wait anymore, so I thanked him and tore across campus past the statue of St. Rita (I crossed myself) to South 12th and then Wharton. It was a hot, steamy morning, and by the time I got to Garibaldi Park my shirt was soaked. I slowed down, but that only made sweat pool under my arms and in the small of my back. When I turned onto South Adriana, I saw the cherry tree at Laura's house and stopped short. I hadn't thought about what to say or how to explain what I was doing there. With any luck, though, Big Al would be at work, so at least I wouldn't have to put up with his ragging on me.

I walked up to 305, wiped the sweat from my face, dried my hands on my pants, and rang the bell. Mrs. Fedora came to the door and stood there looking at me like she had absolutely no idea who I was.

"Yes?"

Her voice was kind of hostile. She wore another housedress, red this time, with big white flowers, gardenias or something.

"Missus Fedora, hi, it's Richard, Richard Mercurius. Remember me?"

She scrunched her face.

"I had lunch here last week. I'm Laura's friend from school."

Nothing.

"Queen Elizabeth?" I said, starting to panic.

I thought she was going to slam the door but then she said, "Oh, sure, I remember you now! Come in, Richard. I thought you were one of those goddamn Jesus freaks or magazine salesmen that come around here. We get them all the time.

Laura's still in bed, but you can keep me company while I make breakfast."

She led me into the kitchen, which looked exactly the same. This time, nonno was at the table, holding his head up with one hand and dunking a piece of toast in his coffee with the other. He didn't look up or anything, so I went straight for a chair and slid into it. The only light in the room came from the stove, and the radio with the gold dial was on with the news. Something about a place called Entebbe, which is in Uganda in Africa (I looked it up later on the Rand McNally wall map in my room).

"So, Richard, what brings you out this early?"

"Early?"

I checked the redwood clock on the wall. It was nine-fifteen. "Well, I work at the Day Camp at school and I had to run an errand near Garibaldi Park, so I thought I'd stop by."

"That's nice that you can do that. Are you hungry?"

"A little."

"A little?"

"A lot."

"Good, you can have breakfast with us. In the meantime, I'll get lazy Laura out of bed. That girl would sleep forever if I let her."

She left the kitchen and those words danced in my head like sugarplums: *that girl would sleep forever if I let her*. I imagined Laura curled up in a four-poster bed with a frilly pink canopy, and I started daydreaming. That happens to me a lot. It comes from an active imagination and an overactive sex drive, which is supposed to be healthy for a guy my age, but I don't see how. The only thing I get out of it is sore, if you know what I mean. So, I imagined lying next to her, kissing her hair, rubbing her shoulder, that kind of stuff. We were alone and free to do whatever we wanted. And what I wanted more than anything else was to reach underneath her pajamas and touch her nipple, which I pictured was light-skinned and erect like Michael Corleone's Sicilian bride on their wedding night before she blew herself up in the car reciting her English lesson: *Mon-day, Tu-es-day, Wed-nes-day, Tu-es-day*...BOOM! I imagined inching ever so slowly toward my goal, making my way underneath Laura's pajamas toward her nipple, which waited for the tip of my trembling finger. It was incredible. Then, turning toward me ever so gently in a soft and flowing voice, she screamed—

"BUON GIORNO!"

I nearly leapt out of the chair. I looked up to see nonno's face staring back at me. He had coffee dripping from the end of his nose and toast smeared on his chin. For an instant, I didn't know where I was.

"Buon giorno!" he repeated.

"B-Buon giorno."

Then he held up two fingers and waited.

"Buon giorno...buon giorno," I said.

He didn't move, still holding up the fingers. I didn't know what to do, so I waved two fingers back. He tried to say something, but it was garbled. I nodded and looked away, hoping that would take care of it, but he mumbled again. This time it must have been a question, cause I could tell he expected an answer, those watery blue eyes fixed on me. For the life of me, I still didn't know what he wanted.

"I dunno, nonno, I'm sorry."

For some reason that worked and he sunk his head back over his coffee like he was praying. I started wondering what the hell I was doing there. I mean, this was crazy. What if Laura didn't like me and here I was sitting in her kitchen with this old guy because her mother got off on the royal family with all those dukes and duchesses and earls and pearls? And what if she already had a boyfriend? I never even asked her. I just figured she was interested in me, but she could have stopped by yesterday just to be nice. Some girls were like that. I looked back at nonno, who looked about as messed up as me, and immediately sympathized with the guy.

Funny, but we had something in common: we were both waiting for Fedora women.

"She'll be down in a minute, Richard," Mrs. Fedora said, coming back into the kitchen, her fuzzy slippers slapping the tile. I hadn't notice them before. Then, her voice lowered, she said, "I see you've met my father-in-law."

"He's been trying to tell me something. He keeps holding two fingers up and waiting, but I don't know what for."

"He wants his eggs. He has two poached eggs and two slices of toast every morning with his coffee. It's his little ritual."

She yelled at him in Italian, and, although it couldn't have sounded meaner, it settled him down and he grinned. From then on, he didn't say another word, just waited for his eggs, which arrived not much later, at least a lot sooner than Laura did. That gave me and Mrs. Fedora enough time to bond, whether I liked it or not, and I can't say I did. She started with the queen again but then moved to the lack of space in their home and how she wanted to move to the suburbs, "where you can have a real life with a swimming pool and central air." I wondered what kind of life they were living now.

"But you have room for a pool here, don't you?"

She laughed, lit a cigarette, and said, "It's not the same thing. We couldn't possibly put a pool out there. It would be *ugly*." She said the word *ugly* like it was snot.

"I don't suppose you have a pool, do you?"

I shook my head.

"Where do you live?"

"Saint Stephen's near the Traffic Court on Spring Garden. We don't have a pool, but my mom wanted to be close to the German and Hungarian families in the neighborhood, and she knows most of them."

"Do you have any brothers or sisters?"

"A brother."

"Older, younger?"

"Younger."

"And your father, what does he do?"

"He's an inventor."

"An inventor?"

"Yes, he's very famous in Hungary. He has lots of patents there."

"Really, in what?"

"Gravity."

I can lie on a dime. It doesn't take much, cause with a family like mine you have to be ready to lie without even blinking. Most people wouldn't understand unless they also come from a crazy family, so I don't try to explain myself or make excuses anymore. It's useless. Besides, I think Mrs. Fedora was asking for it. She was asking too many questions and getting nosy. Adults do that to make sure you have the right stuff for their daughters, but they also like to dig into your personal life just to test you, maybe come up with crap they can sling at cocktail parties and barbeques. I've seen it happen.

"That's very interesting, Richard," she said. "I bet you have intellectual discussions when you're all together."

"Not really."

"No, why not?"

"Well, my mother's English isn't great even though she works for the phone company, and my father stays in his room on the third floor and doesn't come out much."

"His room?"

"It's his laboratory."

"He sleeps there?"

"No, not all the time. Sometimes he doesn't sleep at all and stays up listening to Glen Campbell records. His favorite song is *Rhinestone Cowboy*."

I paused for a few seconds and then sang as innocent as could be, "You know, '*getting cards and letters from people I don't even know.*' I guess he wants to be famous from his inventions and stuff."

"In gravity?"

"Right."

She stared at me, trying to decide if it was a crock or not, fired a barrel of blue smoke out her nostrils, and kept staring. Finally, Laura came thumping down the stairs into the kitchen. She wore a dark blouse open two buttons from the neck with white tennis shorts, and her hair bounced around in a ponytail.

"Long time no see," she said to me.

"Hi."

"Laura, breakfast is on the stove. There's enough for the two of you. When you're done, don't forget to clean up," Mrs. Fedora said.

"Where are you going?"

"Downstairs to clean up the mess your grandfather made this morning."

"What happened?"

"I don't want to talk about it. I'm too upset."

"Okay."

"You know that majolica fruit bowl, the one Aunt Connie brought back from Faenza? The old man filled it with grapefruit and snuck it downstairs. Then he dropped it on the floor and smashed it. I swear he does things to spite me. I'm just sick over the whole thing!"

She rushed out of the kitchen with her slippers slapping the floor. Of course, I wasn't paying attention, so I couldn't answer Laura when she asked me if I had seen nonno or not. I honestly couldn't remember. All I could see were the unfastened buttons on her blouse and her legs that flowed like milk into her leather sandals.

"I'm pretty sure I saw him," I said, swallowing. "I mean, yes, I definitely saw him right over there."

I pointed to the chair where nonno had been sitting, and she looked at me like I was speaking Greek, which I actually thought about taking in college—Ancient Greek to complement

Latin—until Mrs. Dudoit said that one dead language was enough. "Stick to the living, Richard," she told me. I decided to take her advice, not because there was no future or money in the Classics, but because whenever she said my name it rhymed with *en guarde!*

"I'm sure he's all right. I worry about him too much," Laura said. "Do you want some coffee? It's espresso."

"Sure."

"My father says it puts hair on your chest."

"It does?"

"He says real men have hair on their chest."

I didn't say anything, hoping this wasn't going where I thought it was going. And then it went there.

"So, do you have hair on your chest?" she asked.

"What?"

"I guess that's a personal thing to ask, so if you don't want to answer, that's okay, I'll understand. Enz has hair on his chest. I've seen it, but then he's older than you. Sometimes he even lets me shave him."

"You shave his chest?"

"No, silly, his face."

I must have looked stunned, because she turned away and pretended to do something at the stove. Thank God the radio was on. The temperature was 86 degrees, humidity was 97 percent, and winds were out of the northeast at ten miles per hour. Inside the kitchen, though, there wasn't any breeze. The room was so heavy it felt like bed sheets when you take them out of the washer and have to get them through that porthole of a dryer door.

"You know, I'm not so hungry after all," she said. "I think I'll just have some espresso and biscotti. How about you?"

"That's fine."

"Come on, we'll eat out back."

She led me to a wrought iron patio table in the yard that had plastic placemats with big golden sunflowers on them. I thought about her shaving Enz and wasn't sure if it turned me on or grossed me out. It was too weird for a brother and sister to be doing, but it was also one of the sexiest things I've ever heard. What got me was the chest hair, though. We're all trying to grow hair like that, so I'm kind of sensitive about it.

I'll never forget going to the barber for my last haircut and telling the guy as nice as could be to leave the sideburns. He stepped back and, in a voice that made everybody in the room look up, said, "Kid, there's nuttin to leave, believe me!"

I couldn't have been more embarrassed and left as soon as I could. Now, the embarrassment continued with Laura. She must have had an older boyfriend with plenty of hair in all the right places.

"I'd better get back to work," I said after a while.

"Do you have to go?"

"Yeah, they're expecting me, but thanks for the espresso and biscotti."

"My mother made them."

"They were great."

Then, as I got up to leave, she said, "Don't you want to see the fig tree? You can see the figs no problem now."

I had no idea what she was talking about but followed her to the tree anyway, which was huge with drooping leaves and silver branches. Underneath, it was cooler and smelled of freshly-shoveled dirt, which was nice. I looked around and saw discolored balls of fruit hanging all around us, which reminded me of gym class, but I tried not to think about that. It would have been too hard to explain.

"So?" she asked.

"So what?"

"Your chest hair, let's see it."

"You're kidding, right?"

"No. What do you think we came out here for--Yahtzee?"

I stared at her. The thing about the St. Rita polo shirt is that there are two buttons at the neck that all the guys leave open to show off their hair, which none of us has except for Bobby Fiore, who also has a mustache and a GTO. The rest of us are as bare as nonno's grapefruits, so at first I wasn't sure what to do but ended up lifting my shirt. What choice did I have, really? If I had said no she would have thought I was hiding something or, worse, a prude. It'd get all over school and my life would be over. So she leaned into my bare chest while I studied the hair follicles in her scalp. She waited a while and then ran her fingers across my skin, laying her palm flat against my heart, which was about to explode. I can't say positively, but I'm pretty sure I wasn't breathing. I couldn't believe this was happening.

"Not bad," she said. "You've got some coming in, I can tell. It'll be a while, but it's definitely there." Then she took her hand away and kissed the spot right over my heart, her lips softly touching, almost grazing my skin.

"Well, that's that. I'll see you around, Merk!"

I staggered out from under the tree like Joe Frazier, stumbled across the yard, down the hall, through the kitchen, and out the front door with the "F." I didn't even notice Mrs. Fedora standing in the hall with broken pieces of fruit bowl in her hands until I was halfway down the street. She might have said something like, "Goodbye, Robert," but I can't say for sure. I had just had my first romantic encounter ever, and it was with Laura Fedora, the car dealer's daughter, under a fig tree at 305 South Adriana Street!

Thursday, July 1

Okay, I've calmed down now. What happened under that fig tree is so unbelievable I have to write about it. That's the only thing I can do, being a writer and all. I could run sprints, but it just wouldn't be the same. I sat down and started doodling, which is what I do when I don't know what else to do. It gets me focused. First, it was lines and circles, boxes and spheres in the margins (next to Brenda's butt), but the more I thought about Laura, the more I wanted to describe her. So I wrote her name like a million times, each time bigger and bigger, adding more to the "L," which got me thinking about words that start with "L" to describe her and how she kissed my chest with those lips that were as soft and cool as figs. I swear I'll never forget it for as long as I live. That kind of thing doesn't happen every day, at least not to me, so I want it to last forever.

Laura the Liar. That's right, that's my first word for her, which may sound strange considering everything that's happened, but that's exactly why I chose it—I considered everything that's happened. I picked it from all the possibilities like "lazy" (her mom's word) as in lying in bed and making me wait for her, "lucky" as in her getting the lead article when all the time it was meant for me, and "lovely" as in her feet, hair, and everything else about her that makes me turn inside out. It took me a while to figure out, but I finally picked "liar." A good question would be, "Merk, how can you talk about your girl like that?" It may seem crazy, and it's not like I wish we'd never met or anything, but I figure cool reason must prevail. That's the only way to make sense out of what happened. That's how the Romans did things, *sobrietas* and all that, and they conquered the world. So, I've been thinking about how she lied to me not once but a lot. How, you ask? Let me count the ways.

First, she lied about the fig tree. It could have been a lot worse what with no hair and all and it was a terrific turn-on (I had to go home and finish the job), but the fact is she still lied to me. Sure, I lie and daydream and do stuff like that all the time, but at least I admit it. I don't pretend. And I don't go around manipulating people, either. I don't mind, she can manipulate me till the cows come home (mom says that a lot), but it made me feel strange. I mean, *her* nipples were supposed to get hard, not mine. How embarrassing is that? You could say I made the whole thing up about going over to her house, so I was lying, too, and don't have room to talk, which is true, but that's not the point. She shouldn't have done it. It wasn't right. It bothered me as much as the story about her shaving her brother, which I liked but didn't. It was sort of like those sweet and sour dishes at Ming's where we go for dinner once in a while for their Tuesday Specials. Funny thing is, they're not sweet and *then* sour or even sour and then sweet, but sweet and sour *at the same time.* That's what it was like, honest to God.

Second, the girl is a liar, cause she still hasn't told me what's going on, if she has a boyfriend or not. Sometimes she acts like it, like she's way out of my league, and other times she can be sweet like when she sticks up for me with her family. She hasn't said anything to me yet, so how am I supposed to know? If she has a boyfriend, somebody with hair like Bobby Fiore, then what the hell was she doing with me under that tree? I can't figure her out, although it might be that girls are just different and I should shut up and be grateful. I am grateful, especially if it leads to more kissing and stuff, but I'd just like to know what's going on, that's all. And what if she really is dating a Neanderthal? I'll flirt with her as much as possible before getting my ass kicked, that's what. If that's what she's doing, it would be cruel, but that's another word entirely, and it doesn't even begin with "L," so I can't talk about it now. Maybe later.

Third, let's not forget how this whole thing started: she stole my article right out from under my nose and never said a word about it. How could she do that if she wasn't a big-time liar? Answer me that. You can't, because there is no answer. There's no defense, either, so unless she's the cruelest person in the world, which she might be—I'm not ruling it out—she has to give me my assignment back. That's the honorable thing to do. That'll never happen, though, because she already got me to swear that I'm not interested in it, even though I've been thinking about nothing else since last spring when they announced there would be a new vice principal and Glenn gave me the assignment. Am I just supposed to forget about it and let her walk all over me? Is that what she expects or what having a girlfriend is like? Because if it is, I'm not sure it's worth it even with her feet and everything. I just can't believe God would let something like this happen to a guy like me. I'm decent enough, never did anything cruel to little kids or cats. OK, my brother, sure, but that's different.

Fourth and most important of all, Laura did something to me and now I don't even want the stupid assignment back. I don't know what she did or how she did it—Female Black Magic or something—but I don't care about it anymore. I got all worked up and now it doesn't mean anything to me except maybe a ding to my pride, which I'll get over soon enough. But the point is she changed me. I'm not the same guy I used to be and I have this feeling I can't go back no matter what I do. I'm not sure I want to go back and that bothers me even more. It's like I don't know who I am anymore and can't think of anything but her feet and that plum of a derriere that called out to me in French sing-song, *"Ree-chard, Ree-chard, viens m'embrasser, viens m'embrasser/Richard, Richard, come kiss me, come kiss me !"* And I almost did. I wanted with all my heart and I swear I almost did. No matter that Big Al would have crushed my head the way he crushed my hand. Death would have been a small price to pay for the chance to bite into Laura's plum, lick it, sniff it, adore it. Speaking of which, the other day I heard Mark Schmidt tell the guys that Darlene DeAngelo in AP History has an ass so sweet he'd eat her turd. When I heard that I laughed my head off.

So, there are four reasons right off the bat, and I haven't even said a word about *how* Laura lies, which is really something. She gets this look on her face like what she's telling you is the most important thing in the world and a secret that you have to guard with your life. I don't know how she does it, except that I want to believe her. I want to believe every word even when I don't believe a single thing she says. Is that being rotten? Am I a louse? She's got a willing audience, cause I'm so distracted by the thought of rubbing myself all over her that I can't think of anything else. I guess it's easy to lie to someone when they're not paying attention, which is screwy, because all this time I thought I was paying attention, but I still have to wait a day or two before I get what's really going on. Even then there's no guarantee. Seems as if my whole world got turned upside down like one of mom's pineapple upside down cakes. That's it! My first novel is going to be called *My Life as a Pineapple Upside Down Cake.*

I don't know, maybe there's something wrong with me. I've never heard of this before, being full on obsessed about feet and behinds and a pivot in the grass and the smell of espresso. Maybe thinking about her and doing that other thing that I don't want to say all the time are not normal. I've heard guys talk, sure, but not like this and not about a girl's feet. I can't tell anybody, not even Lindeman, who is my best friend in the world but who told me once I have a problem because he caught me smelling my running shoes. See, I wasn't just sniffing or taking a whiff, but really smelling them like they were a glass of wine or something (and this was after practice!). He didn't say a word, just stood there in the locker room at the end of the row shaking his head. I thought everybody had cleared out and I was alone. That could have been the problem, though. Lindeman, I mean. He's really funny and a great guy, but when he moves around he hardly makes a noise and can sneak up on you even when he doesn't mean to. A guy could get punched doing that. One time I almost did. It's annoying as hell.

Maybe I shouldn't blame other people for my quirks. "Idiosyncrasies," Mr. Andrade calls them. I like that word, because it sounds better than quirk, which rhymes with jerk and isn't cool at all. Then again, I've heard of guys named Turk and Dirk, so maybe it's not so bad. I should probably admit that I smell socks, too, wet ones in the winter that mom puts on the radiator to dry. They have a warm, steamy smell that's not half bad, like baked bread. What else would you do with them? It seems perfectly normal to me, which is a word I don't use much, mainly because my life is about as far from normal as you can get. I'm not sure how it got that way except I was born into it and you can't do anything about your family other than pretend you're somebody else, which I do a lot, like when mom sends me to Pantry Pride for groceries. I pretend I'm from another country and make up an accent. It's pretty cool fooling people like that. If they ever found out I guess I'd be in trouble, but, seriously, how would that happen—somebody from "New Calcedonia" shows up in frozen foods and asks for a translator and a price check on the Brussels sprouts? It's just that you have to stay serious and not crack up or you'll give it away. Anyway, with that kind of life it makes perfect sense that this redheaded girl has elbowed her way into it. I just wonder how long it will last, this not knowing and not being able to see her except when I make up some bogus excuse about being in the neighborhood. But how many times can they send me on an errand near South Adriana Street? What was I supposed to be picking up, anyway, pushrods for the Corvair?

Saturday, July 3

Okay, something so incredible happened that I have to write about it. In fact, I still can't believe it. Laura asked me to go with her and her family to Valley Forge to watch the fireworks tomorrow! Even President Ford will be there. So now I'm thinking she doesn't have a boyfriend and maybe even *I* am her boyfriend. She wouldn't have invited me otherwise, right? Maybe she isn't a liar after all, maybe she was telling the truth in some way that I couldn't decipher. There'll be a bunch of people there from St. Rita's, so the pressure is on. I have to figure out what to wear and how much money to take. I don't have much, but I have to take something. What if she wants to buy a souvenir or something or go on a donkey ride? I can't be cheap in front of everybody. I'll buy her a George Washington keychain or a tri-cornered velvet hat. She'll look cool. I just can't freak out about it right now, because I have to keep my eye on the ball. I never in my wildest dreams thought this would happen. Of course, there's a catch. There always is, right? Mom told me I could go only if I took Kornél. He'd love to see the fireworks and it would be good for me to spend time with my little brother. I just about had a heart attack and she must have realized what it would be like with my friends around, so she said I could go but I have to take him to work with me next week. I said sure, anything. I don't care. I mean, it would have been a complete disaster, especially with Enz in the background smirking and wisecracking.

This is a dilemma, except maybe it's not really a dilemma if you think about it, because Laura's going to meet Kornél sooner or later, if not tomorrow, then probably at the Day Camp. Maybe it won't be so bad. It's not like he's dangerous or anything, and from what I've seen he's no worse than nonno. He's younger and doesn't spit up all the time, which is a huge plus. Besides, I decided long ago not to worry about what he might do. I figure people are either going to accept him or they're not. I can't do anything about it. Adults are usually cool about that sort of thing, anyway, since they have their own problems. They wouldn't stand there and make fun of a retarded kid or anything like that. And it's not like he's retarded, because he's not. He can be smart when he wants to. It's just that he acts strange around other people, especially ones he doesn't know. But there are plenty of adults that do that, too. The only difference is Kornél has to take medication for it.

And as far as Laura goes, I have a confession to make, since I've been thinking about it for a while now. Apart from wanting to eat figs with her naked in the garage behind her house and make love in the heat, I don't know what love is, not really. I know I have one thing on my mind, one thing that I have to do, but it feels like the entire world is out to stop me from doing it. So, it's a matter of will, as in whose is stronger, mine or everybody else's. Without getting lame, it's like *Romeo and Juliet* all over again, which we read in eighth grade and watched in class. Romeo says something about the two of them against the world and how nobody else could understand what they're feeling because it's so intense, so *personal*. He doesn't come right out and say that, what with it being Elizabethan English and everybody's in leotards and capes, but you get the idea. It was loud and clear, although a grown-up could watch the same movie and come away with something really different. I'm just glad I used the "L" in her name for Liar, because if I had to talk about love or Love or LUV, I'd end up vomiting. I might do it anyway, I'm so nervous.

Monday, July 5
Fireworks

Something happened up at Valley Forge that has to do with love or maybe its opposite, which I don't think is hate. It didn't really happen as much as I figured it out later while everybody else was looking up at the sizzling fireworks and puffs of smoke. It was even more of a shock than Laura inviting me. See, I realized that the Fedoras are not happy people. I don't know how to explain it except that their needling and teasing all the time isn't an act. I thought it was but now I know it's real. I can't say why, but it's definitely there. Being incredibly thin-skinned, everything gets under their skin, even stuff that has no business being there. I realized it by watching them while they were quiet, which was a first, believe me. Usually, somebody's yelling at somebody else about something or other that I don't have a clue about. You have to be careful, because otherwise you could end up in a minefield. I'll have to think about what it does to Laura. It has to be hard for her, which explains why she always sides with nonno.

Anyway, the usual people were there, mostly friends of Laura like Samantha Valentine (her real name), Kathy Schwarzkopf—aka Kate Scheisskopf (from *Catch 22*)—Laurie DeAngelo (Darlene's younger sister), Jenny Mancuso and her brother, Chris (varsity wrestling), this girl on *The Review* whose name I forgot but who has braces and plays the flute in the jazz band, and, of course, Brenda-Big-Butt Conti. Laura was the most beautiful of them all. She brought her feet along, too, and I made sure they were in full view all the time, which wasn't easy what with picnic tables and chairs and people standing around. There was also this other family there, friends of Mrs. Fedora. They came to see the covered wagons that had traveled all the way from Oregon or someplace like that where Lewis and Clark had been. They yelled and made a racket but had great snacks and plenty of different colored sizzlers. They also had two little kids that ran around screaming and poking everybody in the ass with the tips of American flags. Enz brought one of his buddies along, a guy in a rock band with purple hair dressed in black. Nonno sat in a lawn chair wrapped in blankets like it was cold or something and sipped this drink called "grappa," which they made me try and as far as I could tell was a mixture of hydrochloric acid and grain alcohol. When I choked and spit it out they laughed, which is another reason I know they're miserable: they love it when other people get burned, mainly me, but they'll take anyone who comes along. It's like the spider and the fly. They were about to pounce on Purple Head, but Enz stuck up for him so they left him alone.

After I spat up, things settled down. Laura spent a lot of time with her friends, which made me wonder again what the hell was going on. It got me thinking about love, not Figgy Love or *Romeo and Juliet* love but that other kind, the one adults tell you is the real thing, like Coke. But if it really exists, I haven't seen it, not at my house or Laura's or anywhere else. A perfect example is what happened not long after we got there. There was this lady, one of the salesmen from Big Al's dealership, who came up for the barbeque and fireworks. She wore a straw hat with a black band and was with two other salesmen but spent most of the time stuck to Big Al like gum on his shoe, which was strange considering he looks like a Wishnik doll and Mrs. Fedora kept giving her the Zulu eye the whole time. The nice thing was that it deflected attention away from the rest of us so we could do whatever we wanted, which was mainly to hang out in little groups and say stupid things, with Laura completely ignoring me. I thought about pelting her with marshmallows but didn't. Anyway, this woman kept glomming onto Big Al and asking ridiculous questions like was there really a forge in the valley and what kind of tree was that over there and did the troops really drink their own piss, at which point Mrs. Fedora said that she was mixing up survival stories and nobody in the Continental Army ever drank piss. The woman smiled this fake little smile and then went back to Big Al, leaving him only for a bathroom break, which she took in one of those green Port-a-Potties, taking her plastic cup of Chablis with her. It must have been really hot inside, and there's no way of washing your hands.

"Al, what is *she* doing here?" Mrs. Fedora said, not bothering to wait for the woman to disappear behind the green door.

"What are you talking about?"

"You know what I'm talking about."

"Summer? She's just one of the guys. Besides, she's got nowhere else to go, so I said she could join us."

"One of the guys?"

"She's harmless."

"And *Summer*, what kind of name is that?"

"Jesus, Rose, it's just a name. How should I know?"

"I think you know more than you're telling me."

"Look, I don't want to do this now, not in front of everybody. We came up here to have a good time, so why don't you just take it easy for a while?"

"It looks like Summer will take it any way she can get it."

"Rose, don't start."

"Start? You're the one who started it, but I'll finish it, I'm telling you."

"There's nothing to finish. Come on, have a burger or something. I'll put extra cheese on it. You'll like it."

"What?"

"You heard me, extra cheese."

"Don't patronize me!"

"Who's patronizing you? I'm just telling you to calm down."

"And don't tell me to calm down. You've got some nerve bringing her up here, especially when we've got guests."

"I don't know what the fuck you're talking about! All I did was tell her she was welcome along with the rest of the guys."

Mrs. Fedora looked over at me, Laura, and Brenda. The three of us must have been staring back like deer. "Watch your language," she said calmly.

"Goddamn it, this is ridiculous!"

"I said watch your language!"

"Yeah, okay."

"And I'll tell you what's ridiculous—me standing here talking to you."

At that, Mrs. Fedora stormed off toward the parking lot.[4] She weaved her way through the cars and across the parking lot to the horse trail where the wagon train was. Maybe she figured she could get sympathy from the pioneer women who had to travel

---

4 *Estne uxor laeta? Minime! (Is the wife happy? Not at all!). See my drawing of Rose walking off and the green Port-a-Potty. I don't know the word for "pissed" in Latin. If I asked Mr. Elias, our Latin teacher, he'd probably make me decline it. I'm thinking it's a third or fourth declension adjective.*

thousands of miles across the country with their own versions of Big Al and Summer. Of course, everybody knows real pioneer women would have just conked their men out with a frying pan and buried them under a rock somewhere in the Mojave Desert. Big Al sure as hell deserved it. He was eating up the attention from Summer big time.

"Where's she going?" I asked.

"I don't know," Laura said. "But if she keeps walking that way she'll end up on the other side of Mount Joy."

"What's over there?"

"Mount Misery."

"You're joking."

"Didn't you read the brochure?"

"There's a brochure?"

"One of those women dressed like Martha Washington was handing them out."

I remembered the woman. She was fat and had a pinched face as red as a cabbage. I felt sorry for her, because she looked like she was about to explode in the heat.

"Do they do this a lot?" I asked.

"Do what?"

I looked at her.

"Oh, you mean the arguing. Sure, all the time, but that's just the way they are. I don't pay much attention to it anymore."

"How do you do that?"

"I don't know. I just do"

"I don't get it."

"There's nothing to get. Some people are like that and that's all there is to it. What are you, Joyce Brothers all of a sudden?"

Brenda giggled.

"No, I just meant that—"

"Forget it," she said. "Let's go for a hike."

"Now?"

"Why not?"

"It's kinda hot."

"You afraid of melting?"

"No."

"Then let's go."

Another thing about Laura is that she's always going somewhere. She comes up with these ideas mid-sentence and then we're off just like that, which I actually like. She's spontaneous that way, whereas I'm into planning everything, mainly because at my house nothing gets planned. So I plan every little detail like which side of the steps to walk on when I go upstairs at night to bed. I want to make sure I spend an equal amount of time on both sides of each step so that over time they wear evenly. It's just a thing I do, you know, to even things out. I feel better when everything is evened out.

I was surprised when Brenda didn't tag along. Probably wouldn't have made it with that big butt of hers, anyway. It was just me and Laura walking through crowds of people across a hot asphalt road that was soft from the heat to "Redoubt 3." When we got there we sat under a willow tree, where it was cool and shady. I was drenched with sweat and it was running down my face like water, which, technically, it was. I could hardly breathe, but I was with Laura, so what did I care about breathing? I would have drunk my own piss to be with her. After a while it got quiet and all we could hear were voices echoing from over at the picnic area. Laura whispered, "Merk, don't you want to kiss me?" I just about wet myself. She must have had a thing for trees or something, which was fine by me.

"You mean it?"

"If you don't want to, that's all right."

"No, really, I do."

There was this pause like she was waiting for me to do something, so I leaned into her, my lips scrunched for the big one, but she pushed me back and said, "No, not here. There are too many people."

"What?"

"Too many people," she repeated.

I looked around but didn't see anybody maybe within a hundred miles. Not a soul. The closest people were on the other side of the road, and past them was the parking lot. I had no idea what she was talking about.

"Then where?"

"How about there?"

She pointed to another tree, this one a huge, dark walnut at the bottom of Mount Joy, which I figured was a good omen. It was green and leafy and shimmered in the heat like a mirage. I could already feel joy spreading through me.

"Well, it doesn't look like there's anybody over there," I said.

"I'll race you!"

And she was off again, faster than I expected—a lot faster— but as a sprinter I couldn't let her win, even if we were just horsing around. I have a reputation to protect. So, I bolted into the heat and across the open field till I was matching her stride for stride. She tried as hard as she could to beat me, but I was too fast and burst ahead of her, arms and legs pumping. Once I started I couldn't help myself. I get competitive that way. Just ask anybody on the track team. I got there at least twenty seconds ahead of her, maybe more. When she reached the tree she came running up and rammed me with her head before I could catch my breath. I tripped over a huge root and lay sprawled out with a foot in the air.

"Hey, what the hell did you do that for?" I yelled, dirt clinging to my sweaty arms and new blue shorts.

"No reason. Just felt like it."

"What, are you crazy?"

"No."

"Then you're a sore loser," I said.

"I'm not a sore loser. You're just stuffy and don't like to get dirty!"

"*Stuffy?*"

"That's right."

"Am not."

"Are, too."

"Am not."

"Are, too."

"Am not!"

"Are, too!"

You get the idea. It would have gone on like this forever (it reminded me of tennis), so I lunged forward in all my stuffiness and wrestled her to the ground—the girl even tried to bite me!—and that's when it happened. Well, to tell you the truth, it didn't but should have, that magic moment I have been thinking about ever since I saw her foot dangling like a participle in Mr. Andrade's office. *That magic moment so different and so new, was like any other until I kissed you.* But just at that moment, who should show up all out of breath and panting but Kate Scheisskopf and Big Butt, having been sent to look for us by none other than two-timing Big Al.

"You're in big trouble," Brenda said to me, her ugly face all red and swollen. The two of them stood over us.

"What for?"

"Running off without telling anybody where you were going."

"We weren't going anywhere. It's not like we had a plan. Besides, what do you care?"

"I don't."

"Good."

"Except that I want to see you get yelled at."

"Nobody's getting yelled at," Laura said, getting up and brushing herself off. "We just went for a hike."

"Well, your father sent us to get you. The burgers are done."

"Where's my mom?"

"I don't know. She didn't come back."

Without a word, the four of us trudged back in the heat. Laura, Brenda, and Kathy were ahead of me, and I brought up the rear, which was exactly what I watched the whole time: their rears. Kathy's was bony and pale, Brenda's swayed like a horse trailer, but Laura's was delicious. When we got back to the picnic area it turned out to be no big deal, since Chris and Flute Girl had also disappeared—*ooh, la, la*—and Mrs. Fedora was still MIA. In fact, I figured out that the real problem was that Big Al didn't want to be alone. The salesmen and Summer had gone off to the Memorial Arch, leaving him alone with nonno. I thought about asking him if he missed me but then decided not to say anything. On another episode of *Wild Kingdom*, I remember them saying how you should always respect nature, because just when you think you're safe and let your guard down, a python comes along and wraps itself around your ankles and crushes your bones.[5] And, let's face it. Big Al is more dangerous than a python.

---

5 *I heard once that some guy's pet python got loose and wrapped itself around a toilet bowl and cracked it. Okay, maybe that didn't really happen, but who has a python for a pet except somebody in the circus? Or the Philadelphia Folk Festival?*

Things got boring again until Mrs. Fedora came back. I thought there'd be this huge fight between them. You know, flying cheeseburgers instead of toast, but there wasn't. Just a lot of smoldering politeness and ignoring each other through the rockets' red glare and the smell of gunpowder. I wouldn't want to cross either one of them, that's for sure. But you could tell that each knew exactly where the other one was and what they were doing. It's like they were following each other without looking, like they had eyes in the back of their heads or some kind of radar. Marriage Radar. They needed it with all the boom-puff of the fireworks. Laura didn't talk to me the rest of the night, either, but I was okay with that, because I could tell she was watching me, following me without looking. We were doing the same thing as her parents, which should have been incredibly scary but wasn't. It was like our own version of Marriage Radar. Figgy Radar. It felt like we were all grown-up. Boom-puff, boom-puff, boom-puff, sizzle!

Thursday, July 8

I tried calling her the next day (you know, cause I'm obsessed). I got her number from a guy who knew another guy who had taken auto shop with Enz and still had the Fedoras' phone number, but after all that all I got was nonno's raspy voice and the phone hitting the floor, so I left it alone. I figured if it was that hard, it wasn't meant to be, which got me thinking about "meant to be" and life in general. I mean, if something's so hard that you never do it, does that mean it wasn't meant to be? It's not like I don't believe in God or anything like that, but meant to be according to whom (dative case)?

"God, that's who," Fr. Szemeredi said one Sunday after Mass at St. Stephen's. "Saint Paul tells us in Ephesians that God has a plan for each one of us."

"Me, too?"

"Of course, Richard. Your job is to find out what it is."

"It is?"

"Yes."

"How do I do that?"

"I'd say the best way is by listening."

"Listening?"

"That's right."

"But I listen all the time."

"You do?"

"What?"

All right, so I'm listening now. I've been listening for a while, but so far nothing. If God's plan was for me to meet Laura Fedora, then why is it so hard talking to her? And why are things so complicated, with her being sneaky and me trying to get into her pants all the time with no freakin success? It doesn't make any sense. The more I think about it, the more I'm convinced that life is hard like Advanced Trigonometry and if you're going to get anywhere, you can't worry about the hurdles. You just have to try your best and forget meant to be. You can't think about it or you'll go mental. On the other hand, when do you give up and throw in the towel? Do you fail Advanced Trig three times? I'm serious. I'm thinking about taking it next year. This is driving me crazy, because I don't care about sacrificing myself on the altar of NEVER SURRENDER and all that, but when does Do-or-Die become Kamikaze Krazy? I don't want to go on any suicide missions, even for the Most Delicious Derry Derriere in South Philly.

After work today I took the bus home without going to Laura's. I wasn't in the mood for Big Al and the queen's hats and all that yelling. Also, I don't know how Laura feels, but I'm still trying to sort things out. It's all this tree stuff that I don't understand, from figs to walnuts. Maybe we're so different that I'll never figure her out, which makes the whole thing seem ridiculous. I mean, why do things have to be like this? Is it just to make people suffer? Why would God let that happen? I guess I don't get a lot of things and, worse, when I think of all the work I'll have to do to figure it out, I just want to vomit. Anyway, I was so disgusted that when I got home I went straight to my room, even running up the middle of the steps. I didn't care. I thought about talking to mom, telling her about Laura, but she's so old she wouldn't understand. Besides, things are different here in modern day Philly. It's not the old country with horse-drawn wagons and castles and vampires. It's also the 1970s, and most people are doing whatever they want and having sex all over the place (not me, but most people). I don't think she'd get it and would probably make me feel ashamed for even bringing it up, which is what she does most of the time.

I didn't know what else to do, so I found Fiji on the map (it's way out there) and then read "M-N" in the *World Book Encyclopedia*. When I got bored reading about the industrial uses of manganese, I went downstairs and found Kornél in the living room playing with the Erector Set dad got him for Christmas, which probably contains manganese.[6] He was so busy he didn't hear me come in. Mom was in the kitchen making dinner, so I sat in the brown armchair with the ragged arms and did nothing. I just looked around the room, which I've never done before. All of a sudden, things looked small and not so nice. Laura's house is a lot nicer. I guess that's because Big Al makes a lot of money at the car dealership, and, seriously, who would argue with him about undercoating? Her living room has a gold couch with a plastic cover and wedding and First Communion pictures on the walls and a gold chandelier that fills the whole room with light like the palace at Versailles. Ours is the dullest you can imagine with a dark rug with a hole, fiberglass drapes that make the place look like a motel in the Pine Barrens, and a coffee table and floor lamp that we bought at the parish bizarre last spring. It's not that I blame dad for being

---

6 *Manganese is used to make stainless steel and bananas have a lot of it. Go figure.*

unemployed (it gives him time to invent antigravity devices). I just wish he'd come down once in a while to talk to me. It might help me figure things out with Laura. Then again, the way things work around here, it might mess them up even more. By the time I finished looking around, Kornél was staring at me, waiting for me to answer a question I hadn't even heard.

"Well?" he asked, looking up from the floor. "What do you think?"

"About what?"

He pointed to something that looked like a skyscraper with a crane on top.

"Not bad," I said.

He smiled. "Better than you can do."

"Maybe, but I don't play with toys anymore."

"It's not a toy, it's serious."

"Okay."

"And you do, too, play with toys, cause you ruined my Silly Putty, remember?"

"Jesus, Kornél, you're not going to start that again, are you? It was an accident for cryin out loud."

"You got dirt in it and ruined it. Now, I can't copy Flattop and Pruneface!"

"Didn't mom buy you another egg?"

He nodded, remembering.

"All right, then."

"You still ruined it," he said.

"Okay, whatever you say. I ruined it."

He went back to his Erector Set and I went back to being annoyed. Sure, I ruined his stupid Silly Putty by throwing it around the street with Lindeman—we were trying to bounce it as high as the telephone pole—but then I started thinking how *he* was ruining *my* life. Things would be a lot different if Kornél weren't my brother and I didn't have to live in a house that was falling apart. I wish I had somebody else's life, somebody who could afford braces and tennis lessons (not that I'd take them, of course). Somebody like Bobby Fiore who could have any girl he wanted just because he's got chest hair and a GTO, like those were the best qualities in a boyfriend. Maybe I'm not tall or strong or rich, but I will be someday. I'm what they call a Late Bloomer. But if I had a different life, maybe I wouldn't be a Late Bloomer. Maybe I'd grow up faster and have gobs of hair and money and could chain smoke cigarettes out in the open. I don't know. I think this is a humongous waste of time and completely stupid. How did I get born into this family, anyway? If this was part of the divine plan, I've got a divine beef with God. I don't care if it gets me in trouble or not. The whole thing is unfair and screwy.

We had dinner, carrots and peas and this spicy meat dish that I like. It's supposed to come with pasta, but mom didn't boil any because she had to work all day at the phone company and was tired. I know what that's like, so I didn't say anything even when she asked me what was wrong and I told her nothing. That was all we said, which was a good thing, because I wasn't in the mood for talking. I thought about calling Laura but never got the chance, since the phone is in the kitchen and there's always somebody stationed next to it. Even when there's nobody there it's dangerous, because you can hear everything from the living room. Besides, I looked around the kitchen while we were eating and saw that it was just as crappy as the rest of the house and nowhere near as nice as Laura's, which has all those nick-nacks and ceramic statues. Not that I'd ever have her over, so it doesn't matter. I'd die if she ever saw where I live or met my family. This thing between us is just that—between us. It's personal, and no one else needs to know about it. When we finally do it, we won't tell anyone. We'll have an afternoon delight in the garage in her yard just like the Starland Vocal Band, and nobody'll be the wiser. God, if mom ever found out it'd be the end of me. Skyrockets in flight or not.

Friday, July 9
Brotherly Love

"Richard, why don't you take Kornél with you today?" mom said at breakfast the next morning right when I was putting a spoonful of Wheaties in my mouth. I choked, which is happening to me a lot lately. The Big 99 was on in the background. It was 74 degrees, overcast, and my life was about to end.

"Today?"

"Why not?"

"I'm not ready. I mean, this isn't the best time. Does it have to be today? Couldn't you give me a warning?"

She gave me a look, which I guess was the warning.

"He can play with the other kids," she said.

"But most of them are little."

"What about the counselors?"

"They're all older."

"Older schmolder. There must be something he can do. He can't stay here all day. He gets bored."

I hid behind the Wheaties box, which had an offer for a "Dave Stockton Golf Ball," whatever that was. I read the coupon three times. When I finished, I got up and put my bowl in the sink. From the window, I could see Kornél in the yard standing over the garbage cans and talking to them like there was somebody inside.

"Richard?" mom said.

I was paralyzed, but I had already given my word, so what was I supposed to do? A promise is a promise.

"Sure, okay."

"Good, I'll make you boys a lunch."

And that was that, end of discussion. Mom's problem solved, mine just beginning. She made two salami sandwiches with Hungarian peppers and *körözött*, a garlic cream cheese, and poured iced tea into a thermos that she had made the day before with a pitcher of water and Lipton tea bags. When she finished, we rode the bus to school. Kornél was so excited he started squirming all over the place, which was annoying as hell, so I had to tell him to calm down or they'd throw us off and we'd have to walk the rest of the way. After that he sat still, holding onto the lunch bag so tight his fist turned red.

"What are you doing?" I asked him, annoyed.

"It's my job," he said.

"If you say so. Just make sure you don't bother anybody when we get to school. You got that?"

"Okay."

The bus took that long ride down Broad Street, and I saw people walking to work and stores opening up and a guy putting coins in a parking meter. I felt bad, because that's all I ever tell Kornél, stop bothering people. What I really mean is stop bothering me, because I have things to do and a life to lead and you're a major embarrassment. That's a pretty rotten thing to say, especially to your own brother, but it's the truth. I wish he'd stop pestering me and following me around all the time. If he were normal, it wouldn't be so bad and we could do things together like Lindeman and his kid brother, who go to ballgames and movies and stuff like that. I wish I could be like Lindeman. I don't know why I'm not except maybe I think too much, which shouldn't be a bad thing for a writer, but it doesn't make up for being rotten. Truth is, I hate myself for feeling this way, but what am I supposed to do? I just try not to think about it, which makes me mad. I'm madder than I should be, which pisses me off (what *is* Latin for pissed?). That's probably why Lindeman is the lifeguard and I'm not. I'd blame people for drowning.

"Look, over there!" Kornél yelled when we got to the school-yard and he saw Joanne Conti holding Squiggly and Piggly. Joanne thinks she's all that because she happens to be Brenda's younger sister. She was showing the pigs to some new kid and his mother. Kornél went straight up and started playing with them.

"Are you coming to camp, too?" Joanne asked.

Kornél didn't say anything.

"No, he's my brother," I told her.

"Really?"

"He's here for the day."

"I didn't know you had a brother."

"Well, I do. His name is Kornél."

"Hi, Kornél."

"Hi."

Then she got this grin on her face, the same one I've seen on Brenda except not as fat. Their noses curl up and you can see right into their nostrils. They think they're Allie McGraw. It's pretty disgusting.

"What?"

"Oh, nothing," she said.

"Okay, whatever."

I left them standing there with the pigs and nostrils and the mom and went to the equipment room where at least it was quiet. I put the balls out and set the board games up, including the chess set with all the pieces, even though only a couple of people play, mostly another counselor named Jay who has curly hair and keeps talking about Bobby Fischer and Boris Spassky like they just had a sleepover. Lately, the girls have been playing something with marbles or rocks called "Mancala." I have no idea what it is, and I don't want to know. They roll the rocks around in their sweaty little hands like dice (except they're not dice) and giggle and talk about a hundred miles-an-hour. I don't go out there except to clean up spilled soda or stuff like that. It's their little clubhouse—"No Boys Allowed"—which is fine by me.

Just as I was about to go back to Kornél, Mr. Andrade came over and asked me to fix two busted swings on the playground and clean the slide, which he called a "sliding pond." I said sure but then had to go back to ask him what a sliding pond was. He laughed and said he's from New York and that's what they call it there. Something about the Dutch, "the real Dutch, not the Pennsylvania Dutch, who are really German." I wondered why he talked funny. I just figured it was because he's an English teacher and that's what they do. Same reason he wears loafers. He told me once he has three pairs, all oxblood, honest to God. He said he moved here for Mrs. Andrade, who is from Manayunk and wanted to stay near her family. "Are they real Manayunk or Pennsylvania Manayunk?" I asked him. I thought it was pretty funny, but he just gave me a weird look and walked away. At least he didn't bring up the other day with Laura. I felt glad about that.

By the time I finished everything it was already noon. I didn't see Kornél anywhere, so I went looking for him, expecting the worst and wondering why nobody had complained about him. That's when I found out something incredible. Turns out he was a huge hit. Seriously. All the kids loved him, because he played kickball with them all morning. The counselors, the girls mainly, thought he was cute and asked him all kinds of questions about what it was like living with me. He was decent enough and told them I was the best brother in the world and that I gave him money once to buy a balsa wood airplane. I remember that. It was last spring, and I had given him the money to get rid of him. I was trying to hang out with these guys who took karate lessons instead of regular gym class and were pretty tough. It didn't work out, though, because I spent all my time studying and doing homework while they were in Sean Farrell's basement beating the crap out of each other and playing with nunchucks.

I found him sitting outside the equipment room in the shade, holding the lunch bag as tight as before. Even though he must have been hungry from all that running around, he still waited for me to eat. He hadn't even opened the thermos.

"Hey, Kornél, I hear everybody likes you," I said, sitting down next to him and unscrewing the thermos.

"Yeah."

"How did you manage that?"

"I dunno."

"Well, did you have a good time?"

"Yeah."

"Aren't you thirsty?"

"No, Joanne bought me a Fresca."

"She did?"

"And a Hershey bar with almonds."

"You're kidding."

"Nope."

"She never did that for me."

"She likes me."

"So, you're not hungry?" I asked.

"Maybe."

"You're not sure?"

"I dunno."

There was this pause and I knew something was up. He clams up like that when he gets moody. I wondered if something had happened.

"What's the matter?" I asked.

"Nothing."

"Was anybody mean to you?"

He shook his head.

"What then?"

He looked down and kicked at the ground, squirming the way he does. "It's nice here," he said at last.

"Nice?"

"Yeah."

"What do you mean?"

"I mean I like it here."

"So, what's the problem?"

"You're here but I'm not," he said.

"Me?"

"You."

I didn't say anything, just stared at him. I didn't even know what to say except that I knew what he meant. At least I thought I knew. See, this is my life, and even though I think it's a waste of time, what with Animal Habitat and Joanne Conti and snot-nosed kids, to him it's a big deal. He gets to leave the house and make friends and run around all day. He doesn't have that at home. This is freedom for him, and he gets to be a normal kid. I never thought of it that way before, which means I never looked at things the way he does. I never realized that my getting out of the house meant that he was stuck there, which isn't so bad, except he's a kid and it's not right. After all, it's about right and wrong, right? So, who's to say Kornél shouldn't be here, that he shouldn't get a shot at the life I have, even if it's filled with pig shit? I never thought the life I had was so great until I met Laura, even though it's been like that roller coaster at Wildwood from the moment we met. On the other hand, I don't think Kornél knows how lucky he is. Nobody ever bought me a Hershey bar, especially the Conti sisters.

We ate the salami sandwiches with peppers and cream cheese, and the iced tea was great, cold and not too sweet. We even found cookies in the bag, my favorite—not Oreos, which everybody eats, but Pecan Sandies. Mom must have snuck them in when I was combing my hair for the hundredth time. You never know who you'll run into. The other counselors were all around the yard, and the kids sat at picnic tables under the sycamore tree. Lindeman was at the pool, which was surrounded by a fence with signs warning you that if you drown, St. Rita's couldn't care less and won't pay for the funeral much less medical expenses. Don't even think about it. When we finished, Kornél wanted to ride the swings, so I went with him and stood there, looking in the direction of Laura's house and her yard with the fig tree, hoping she would come by again but not really counting on it. That's how I handle most things. It's all in my head, I guess. It made me depressed.

For the afternoon session, Kornél went to the finger painting station inside the gym where it was cool and quiet. He didn't want to do the water games outside, where the kids ran around screaming and Jimmy Grabowski hosed them down till their clothes were plastered to them. I don't blame him. I stayed inside, too, putting everything in bins and boxes and shelves where they belonged. Some of the kids wanted to play badminton, so I read them the rules and then helped them pair up. But the minute I turned my back I had to go back and extract one of the twerps from the net. I had no idea how he got stuck there, but he looked like a dolphin in a tuna net. Things stayed that way, boring, until five o'clock when the parents came to pick up their kids. They circled the school in their cars, honking. Some came in.

Joanne came up with Kornél and said in that phony way of hers, "It was a pleasure meeting you, Kornél. I really like your artwork. It's nice to know there's at least one sensitive person in the Mercurius family."

"Take a hike, Joanne," I told her.

"You're just jealous."

"Of what? That he spent time with you? You wish."

"No, cause your brother's nicer than you and we like him better."

"I'm crushed."

She stuck her nose up and walked away.

I yelled, "Hey, Joanne, love means never having to say you're sorry!"

"Richard, look at this," Kornél said.

"What is it?"

He held up a huge sheet of art paper smeared with green paint from end to end. It was so heavy the edges flopped over, but I could make out green trees and green birds like peacocks and a huge green blob of sun.

"It's a jungle," he said.

"Yeah, it looks like it."

"I gave it a name."

"You did?"

"Everything has a name, right?"

"I guess so. What's it called?"

"Blue," he said. "I call it blue."

He looked at me, beaming, and all I could do was nod. During the entire bus ride home I never even asked. I thought about it, sure, but I never said a word. Some things you just have to leave alone.

Saturday, July 10

I wrote Laura's number in the back of my journal and on my wall map. I wrote it in the blue Arabian Sea between Bombay in the east and Juwara in the west. I'm pretty sure nobody'll find it there. Hell, I might not find it, so I'm committing it to memory: JA8-0637. I'm trying to figure out the sequence mathematically so it's easier to remember, you know, in case I get a head injury or need to remember it in an emergency, but I'm having a hard time. If I convert JA8 to numerals, 528, that would give me 5280637, which are two three-digit sets of numbers on either side of a zero. Cool. Now, the middle number in the set on the left is even (2) and on the right odd (3), and 2 and 3 are just one number apart, which makes them practically brother and sister. The number to the left of those two middle numbers is the opposite type: an odd number (5) in the left set and an even number (6) in the right set, and 5 and 6 are also one number apart. Even cooler. But the number to the right of the middle number is the same type as the middle number: 8 on the left side, which is even like 2 and 7 on the right, which is odd like 3. All right, so far so good, but I can't get beyond that. I'm stuck. I can't pair the numbers differently, say, by connecting the numbers on the left in both sets (5-6) with the numbers on the right (8-7), even though they are one up (5-6) and one down (8-7), which is the original difference between the two middle numbers (2 and 3) and form a numerical sequence, 5-6-8-7, creating a kind of musical crescendo between the 6 and 8. I could say that one day you're up (5-6) and the next day you're down (8-7), but it's all starting to get confusing, especially when you consider that they're mixed odd and even numbers, odd being masculine and even feminine, which I figured out one day from the shape of 1 and 0. It wasn't hard. Anyway, I guess I shouldn't freak out about it. It's not like I'm going to call her. I wouldn't know what to say.

I know I have to call. I must call. I cannot *not* call. Absolutely no way. Or I'll rot. But I will not rot or I'll get a clot (I've been reading my collection of Doctor Seuss books, which I love almost as much as Danny Dunn). The reason, you see, is that I really don't know what to say, not after all that mathematical permutation. But will I ever see her again? I'm not too sure. I'm not sure about anything anymore except that ever since I met her I've been the most miserable dude in the universe. Is *that* love? If it is, then maybe I can't do it, maybe I haven't got the stomach for it. I guess I'm a coward. Love is like strychnine. Eventually, it will cause my jaw to freeze shut and my urine will turn black like a poisoned rat. I've got poison throughout my body and I'll die soon. She might as well go ahead and do the interview with the vice principal. Would she come to my funeral? Weep and throw herself on my coffin? Throw herself on my coffin and then weep?

Then there's that other thing that's been eating at me and came to a head after getting home from camp yesterday, where all the talk was about Kornél and what a great guy he is (not like his brother). I have to believe that this pain I feel for Laura, if it really is from love and not her mother's cooking (so far everything's been burnt, including the biscotti), comes from the same place that my love for Kornél comes from. That's logical, right? I mean, we're in the City of Brotherly Love and I do love him. He's been like a brother to me. So, why is it that I don't show him any love? Why do I treat him like the biggest pain in the neck there is, even when he's not, which I might even tell him someday? And—here's the biggie—how can I tell Big Al I'm in love with his daughter whom (the genitive) I do not see a lot of, when I'm a louse to my own brother, whom (accusative) I see every day at the breakfast table? How do I do that? How do I do that without getting Saint Rita of Cascia seriously pissed off at me? And that's not something I want to do.[7]

I must be a louse, rotten to the core, and not worth the space I take up on the planet. I don't know what to do about it, though, because you are what you are and it's not like a bird can all of a sudden start swimming. Well, unless it's a penguin or something, but you get the idea. Wait a minute—now that I think about it, why is a penguin a bird if it can't fly? How can that be? It spends all its time swimming, right, even in ice-cold water? But it's not a fish. It doesn't have scales or anything. It's a bird that swims, but it's still a bird, which means that being a bird must be about something other than flying. It has to be, because one of its own not only can't fly

but does the exact opposite of what birds do, which is swim! So, there must be something on the *inside* that makes you what you are and not what you do or look like on the *outside*. Wow, look at that! I did that all by myself! See my penguin drawing in the margin.

But I'm still up the creek, cause even if I stop acting like a louse by swimming instead of flying or flying instead of swimming, or whatever, I'll still be a

---

7 *For our first home basketball game last year against Ignatius Prep, the all-boy Jesuit high school, some kid from the other side painted the St. Rita statue blue and gold, the Iggie colors, and he got mono the next day and almost died. They had to put him on a strict diet for over a year, and he couldn't do anything strenuous like walk around the block or lift a can of paint. Iggie got blown away 115-87. That's the power of St. Rita!*

louse on the inside. Stopping the louse stuff on the *outside* doesn't change who I am on the *inside*. So, what do I do, then? Just start being nice to my brother and leave it at that, because it's the right thing to do? Sure, it's being moral again, but it has nothing what-soever to do with sitting naked with Laura in the garage behind her house. That means my Brotherly Love for Kornél is different from my Figgy Love for Laura, which may not even be love at all but just one Big Woody.

So, where does that leave me? I'm back to the drawing board, square one, top of the first, "Doe-a-Deer-a-Female-Deer," because being nice to Kornél doesn't help me win Laura over one bit. It's like battling two fronts, then, one at home and the other at school, with me in the middle. A pickle in the middle. How did that happen, exactly? I have no idea, but it's making my head spin, because I'm starting to think that love is more like war than it is like love. So either people go to war because they are secretly attracted to each other, which is pretty messed up, or they love each other because deep down they want to keep their friends close but their enemies closer (our neighbor says that all the time, which makes me wonder why she and mom are so close). If any of this is true, then I am completely lost, even more than the time that guy in the park with a ponytail asked me if I was saved.

"From what?" I asked.

I got home two hours later, sweating.

Monday, July 12

The Great Question. That's what I'm calling the thing that has been on my mind for a while now and is driving me so crazy I can't breathe or see straight. Well, maybe that's an exaggeration, but only a little. And the question is this: After everything that's happened between us—the lunch, the fig tree, the walnut tree, the wrestling, the "Merk, don't you want to kiss me?"—after all that, how come we never get to see each other? Why am I always doing things without her and being by myself? It's like I don't have a girlfriend. And why do I feel so lonely that sometimes I just sit on my bed and stare out the window? How can that be? I'd never tell anybody that, but that's what happens. I'm even ashamed to write it down. I only hope nobody reads this before I die. The last time I saw Laura and her twinkle toes was July 4! That's like an eternity. She could have gone off to college by now and started living with her journalism professor. They probably interview each other naked.

So what started out as incredible is not so incredible anymore. In fact, it's the opposite. I'm miserable, because just when I want to see her, when I've figured out that she's for me and I'm for her and somehow we fit together like a package of Ring Dings, which is the most perfect junk food in the world (I like them better than Twinkies), I can't see her. It's been impossible to see her. And the strange thing is, I have no idea why, no idea why just when things ought to be humming along like a finely-tuned V-8 Cobra (talk about pushrods!), I get Enz's crappy Corvair instead. It doesn't make sense, which is something else I'm beginning to figure out: none of this makes sense because it's not supposed to. Things just happen and there is no divine plan or anything like that, and all the stuff they pass off in church and school is a pile of horse manure. Steaming, smelly horse manure. Will I ever tell Fr. Szemeredi that? I don't know, but how could he believe it himself? Isn't he lying to the whole world? So why shouldn't I say something to him? And what about mom and all those old ladies at St. Stephen's? Isn't he pulling a fast one on them just so they'll mop the floor, dust the altar, and polish the candlestick holders? I'll have to think about that. Right now all I know is that my head hurts along with everything else.

Another part of The Great Question is this: if there is no plan or reason to anything, then why shouldn't I do everything possible to get what I want when I want it? That means moving heaven and earth (another of mom's sayings) to win Laura over and force her to love me until she not only wants me but can't live without me because I'm so sexy, smart, witty, funny, handsome, etc., which "should be obvious to the most casual observer" (it actually says that in my Algebra book about asymptotes, which I thought was one of the kings of Ancient Babylon). There'd be no stopping me, right? So maybe that's what I should do. I'll kidnap her and hold her against her will in some desolate place until she breaks down and falls in love with me. But it would have to be more than that. She would have to give up the teasing and playing me for a fool. And she would have to say it, get down on her knees and recite the following:

"Merk, I love you. You are the only one for me, have been the only one, and will be the only one forever and ever. I knew it from the moment you rushed into Mister Andrade's office all hot and sweaty and muscular, and I promise to turn the interview over to you and tell everyone that you alone are capable and worthy of writing it and that I am in awe of your amazing literary talent (not to mention your extraordinary sexual powers). I love you with all my heart from the bowels of my soul."

Something like that, maybe a little less dramatic, although I like the bowels part. Then we kiss and do other stuff, you know, and I let her go back to her family so they don't get upset and form a posse to hunt me down and shoot me in the street like a dog, which they might do anyway just for kicks.

Tuesday, July 13
Connie Mack Attack

Okay, so after work I went over to South Adriana and completely lucked out. Big Al was still at his dealership where he was having a Big Sale or something, and Mrs. Fedora had gone out with Enz to shop at the Italian Market on 9th. Laura and I sat at the patio table out back, the scene of the crime just twenty feet away. Her hair was loose and flowing all over the place as if she had just washed it. It looked terrific, and just looking at her gave me a boner, but it was okay, because I wore my baggy khaki shorts with the pockets, not the tightie blue ones. It feels strange wearing those in public, because I usually get looks, especially on the bus. I don't think she noticed, but I watched to see if she looked down there anyway.

"Wanna go with me and nonno?" she asked.

"Where to?"

"You know the old Connie Mack Stadium on Lehigh?"

"Sure, but you can't get in. It's been closed for ages."

"They're tearing the last of it down today and nonno wants to watch."

"You're kidding."

"Nope, he read about it in the paper. They've been working on it for a while, and this is the last day to see it."

I couldn't believe it. This was as good as sex. I mean, if you can't have sex, the next best thing would be to watch something get demolished. To stand there and watch a ballpark being torn down was the chance of a lifetime.

"Great, let's go!"

"Hang on, we have to wait for Enz to get back. He's driving us."

"Enz?"

She shrugged.

"In the Corvair?"

"Yeah, why?"

"It's supposed to rain later, and if it breaks down again we'll get wet."

"You're serious?" she asked.

"Uh-huh."

She rolled her eyes in that way of hers that can make me feel naked (not the good kind) and then marched inside. So I sat there curling and uncurling the ends of the placemat, trying to decide if I should really kidnap her and hold her in a love lair. Merk's Love Lair. Dick's Love Lair...*She loves me, she loves me not...kidnap her, kidnap* *her not...*After a while I got bored and looked around the yard. Apart from the garage and fig tree, which I knew like the back of my hand, so to speak, I hadn't noticed much else till now. There was another tree at the far end of the yard, a mimosa, I think, with those little pink blossoms that look sticky and Japanese. Its branches curled over the roof of the garage, almost covering it completely. It was a nice little yard, the kind you see all over Philly, except this one was special: it belonged to the girl of my dreams.

Finally, Enz came back and the four of us piled into the Corvair, which had the top up cause, as Enz put it, "it's gonna rain, you know." I looked over at Laura, but she just stuck her tongue out at me. I wanted to sit in the back with her and almost did, but then it didn't work out cause of leg room or knees or some other problem. She sat behind Enz, which wasn't so bad, because I could still turn around from shotgun and look down at her feet and toes. Nonno sat behind me, hacking into a dirty hanky, and I sat there praying he didn't miss. He wore an old Philadelphia Athletics baseball cap and started talking in English (I think it was English) about the ballpark, the team, and a friend of his in the roofing union who knew Connie Mack. Enz turned the radio up and we sped down Broad Street while KC and the Sunshine Band played "Shake Your Booty." He and Laura did all the moves, which I thought was pretty funny until I remembered how she shaved him and then I got jealous.

We found a spot near the ballpark, which was lucky, because it's a black neighborhood now and pretty sketchy. You wouldn't want to walk too far down Somerset or Lehigh or anywhere else with all the drug addicts and hoodlums. People get mugged there all the time and most of the stores are gone. Everybody's leaving the city and moving to places like Conshohocken and King of Prussia, where the air is clean and the sidewalks are made with fresh cement and there are shopping malls with escalators and food courts with neon lights and Slurpee machines. We got out and walked two blocks to the ballpark, but as soon as we turned the corner I just about dropped dead, because it wasn't what I expected. There were bulldozers and a wrecking crane and dump trucks crawling all over the place. They put up a chain link fence around it, too, so you couldn't get close even if you wanted to.

We stood there kind of stunned, and I noticed other people looking the same, nobody talking, the men shuffling here and there and the women standing perfectly still with their hands on their hips, some holding babies. A couple of guys my age were horsing around on the corner opposite us, public school types, loud and obnoxious, which would have been annoying except you couldn't hear them over the grinding, chomping, chewing, and belching of the equipment. It was awful. It was like watching a wounded animal being eaten alive by lions or that scene in *The Old Man and the Sea*, which we had to read this year, when sharks swim right up to the fish and tear chunks of meat off the bone while the old Cuban goes spastic, cursing and shaking his fist. Like those sharks, the men in the machines went about their work like it was just another day, part of the routine. Some even looked bored, which made the whole thing eerie and not at all the next best thing to sex or even holding hands.

Nonno stood still, not saying a word, which made me wonder what was going on with him. I mean, if it spooked me and I didn't know anything about the place, what was he thinking? So, I watched him. He shifted his weight back and forth, propped his eyelids open to see better, and called Laura over. They talked in Italian. At least I think it was Italian. I can't be sure, because everything that comes out of his mouth sounds like a combination of Czech and radio interference. Then Laura pointed to the front of the building where it was rounded with a dome on top, the kind you see in old buildings and black and white films where everybody twitches and walks really fast on streets with trolleys.

"There, do you see it?" she asked, turning toward me and Enz.

"See what?"

"There, right there. Look straight down the front till you get to the bottom of that window and the top of the arch."

"Where?"

"Oh, yeah, I see it now," Enz said, nodding. "It's just below where it says 'Connie Mack Stadium.'"

"See what?"

"The plaque," she said, pointing.

"I don't see anything."

She came over and stood next to me, pointing, but her warm breath and the touch of her skin paralyzed me. "Okay, *look*," she said, pressing into me and turning my face toward the window. Her breasts, round and womanly, fit snuggly against my arm like their being there was—fine, I'll say it—*meant to be.*

I looked, really I did. I strained my eyes and tried as hard as I could, but I don't think I would have seen an elephant if it sat down on the sidewalk in front of me. How could I? Her hair smelled of ginger shampoo, and those breasts set my arm on fire from my shoulder to my fingertips. Even my side was burning. It was like somebody had put hot barbeque coals in my clothes. I had to tell myself to breathe, which wasn't easy, because my throat clogged up and the air got heavy with dust from the demolition.

"Don't tell me you don't see it?"

I stuttered for the second time, which is something I haven't done on a regular basis since I was Kornél's age.

"Well?"

"Oh, *that*," I said, lying. "Sure, I see it now."

"So, what do you think?"

Before I could make a complete ass of myself, Enz cut in. "Shibe Park. That's what they used to call the place maybe a hundred years ago."

"No, not that long ago, just at the turn of the century. Merk, what if we wrote an article about that?"

"About what?"

"Shibe Park. We could start with the demolition and work backwards, telling the story of the park and the team and even describe what the city was like back then. It could be this whole flashback thing. Maybe they'd let us do a series of articles and we could take turns writing them. You could write about the team and I could do a history of the city. I think it would be terrific and Mister Andrade would love it. What do you say?"

All of this was coming at me pretty fast, so all I could say in a squeaky voice was, "Yeah, that's terrific."

"What's wrong?"

"Nothing."

"No, tell me."

"Well, I thought you were working with Brenda on that story."

"This would be after, but in the meantime you could get started on the research."

"Research?"

"On the team."

"Okay. Should I include the queen's hats?" I said stupidly.

She gave me a look.

"You know, I'm trying to be serious and there you go being a smartass again. It's really annoying."

That hurt my feelings. I thought it was funny, but it never seems to work with her. Nothing works with her. Still, I keep doing it because I'm the Merk and I'm a funny guy. Either that or I'm just really retarded.

"Again?" I asked.

"What?"

"You said 'again' like I've done it before."

"Done what before?"

"Be a smartass."

"What?"

"I said—

One of the machines was munching a pile of twisted metal like there was no tomorrow. It drowned out our conversation, so I dropped it. Besides, she was making the same face she made when we first met, like she smelled a fart, which was confusing coming right after the breast thing and all that razzle-dazzle. It was a letdown, too. Then Enz tapped the crap out of a new pack of Marlboros and offered me one. We smoked while Laura went back to nonno, who must have been having a flashback of his own, because he kept pointing at the scoreboard, which had a "Cold-Brewed Ballantine beer" sign and a clock that was stuck at exactly 12:02. Then he took out his handkerchief and started hacking into it like, well, there was no tomorrow. I wondered what was going on at 12:02 that made the clock stop, but I have learned that some things in life you never find answers to and other things you don't want answers to. Still, if you're going to stop a clock, wouldn't you do it at 12:00 or 12:30? Who picks 12:02? Then it hit me. Nobody picked it. They just let it happen.

Before I finished the cigarette, it started to rain, one of those drizzles that doesn't come from above but from the air around you and smells a lot like grease. It was warm as piss, too, which isn't so bad until you get inside and it feels like you're wearing a bathing suit, which reminds me of dreams I have where I'm going around naked but everybody else is dressed up. I act like it's no big deal, but I usually wake up spooked. That's how I feel with Laura. Just when I get comfortable and let my guard down, she drops the kabosh rock and I'm right back where I started. I've noticed girls can do that to you. It's that magic thing again, which I haven't figured out and probably never will. But it's worse than that, because how can you spend your entire life off balance, always on your heels? I don't like that feeling. I also don't want to get to adulthood not knowing who I am or where I'm going. I remember Mrs. Miller in the fifth grade asking us what we wanted to be when we grew up. She asked each one of us, up and down the rows, and when she got to me I told her the truth. I said I didn't know. What I didn't tell her was what a stupid question I thought it was. How the hell should I know, I'm in fifth grade, for chrissakes? But she said if I didn't know then, I'd never know. I think she liked scaring the hell out of us.

We headed back to the car but had to go at nonno's pace, which was a little faster than a blind slug, so we were pretty wet when we got there. Naturally, the classic wouldn't start, so we sat there until something happened to the engine—warmed up, cooled down, dried off, turned over, flipped out—I don't know what, but it probably had something to do with pushrods. When it finally started, Enz drove us to this greasy place called "The Dropsie Cafe" (no lie) where we sat eating bagels and drinking coffee that tasted like boiled swamp mud (not that I've had any, but I can imagine). He knew one of the waitresses there, which was probably the reason he offered to drive us in the first place, so he could see this girl named Deborah who was a premed student at Temple with a bony nose and breasts that drooped like butternut squash (maybe it should have been called The Droopsie Café). She was all right, though, and didn't charge us for the coffee, which was perfect since I only had three bucks and didn't want to look cheap by borrowing money from Enz. Her breasts were nice, too, smooth and tanned. I thought they'd make a hollow sound if you tapped them.

"Hey, Merk, wanna ride home?" Enz asked as we left the cafe.

He was in such a good mood that he was practically whistling, which was annoying, since I wasn't. Laura had ignored me the entire time while she sat eating a pesto bagel and drinking three cups of coffee, heavy on the cream with three packets of sugar. I counted. When a girl has that much cream and sugar, you know she's a lot of work.

"That's all right," I said.

"Come on, we'll drop you off. It's on the way back."

"No, really, I can take the bus from your place."

"He doesn't want us to see where he lives, cause he's got a secret life that we're not supposed to know about," Laura said.

"Really?"

"I think he's a pusher."

"Wow, Merk, can I score a nickel bag?"

They both laughed like my being a pusher was the most ludicrous thing in the world (I guess because I'm too stuffy to be anything but a geek), which irritated me even more. If I could have, I would have walked home.

"Hey, just kiddin, man," Enz said, slapping me on the back. "If you don't want a ride, that's cool."

I didn't want a ride, but I also didn't want to take the bus back, so I was stuck. They ended up driving me, and when we pulled up to 7615 Kingsbury Road, Laura did her best to check it out, craning her neck to look past the chestnut tree in the front yard till I thought she would get a charley horse. Then, because it was raining, she crawled from the backseat into the front without getting out. She can be a real girl sometimes.

"Next time you'll have to invite us in," she said through the cracked window, staring up at me with those endless eyes.

"Okay," I said.

"Promise?"

"Promise."

"Cross your heart?"

I crossed my heart.

"And hope to die?"

I made a face.

"Say it."

"And hope to die."

"Good. Now, if I die first you'll feel really guilty, won't you?"

Before I could answer, Enz turned the radio up again and the classic peeled down the street, fishtailing on the asphalt and disappearing around the corner. I stood there watching it. Then, all of a sudden, I can't explain it, I know I just saw her and she had bothered me so much that I wanted to scream and almost did right there in the street, but I missed her. I really missed her, Laura Fedora. I don't know what happened. Maybe it was that look in her eyes or her hair hanging in clumps or the sound of that wrecking ball, but I got this awful feeling like the bottom of my stomach had just been ripped open and everything I had eaten up to that point was about to come gushing out. It was awful. There's something about saying goodbye that gets to me. Ending things, leaving home, losing sight of the other person, not being with them during the day, waiting on Sunday night for Monday to come, knowing that you have to get up early the next morning—it all gets to me. Drives me out of my skull. Not to mention spending all that time waiting to see her, hear from her, be with her, not knowing what she's doing or who she's with. It's like choking, which I hate more than anything else, even dying.

So maybe I was wrong before and all of this really does mean something; maybe it means a little or maybe a lot, but I'm guessing a lot, because why else would I feel this way? Why would I have these thoughts and feelings that just sit there and do nothing, getting thicker and thicker like Glenn's glasses till I can't see straight? Just for the hell of it? God may be cruel but he's not stupid. This has to mean something. And I'll tell you how I know: tonight they played the All Star Game at Vet Stadium. So, the same day that the old field died, the new one came of age.

National League 7, American League 1. Goodbye, Thurman Munson! Goodbye, cruel world! Goodbye, Yellow Brick Road!

Saturday, July 17

I've been thinking. I know what love is. I finally figured it out, and the strange thing is, the answer has been under my nose all along. It's so obvious. Love is a prowling beast, a Lon Chaney werewolf, a blood-sucking Bela (mom's favorite, because he's Hungarian), a snarling tiger with razor-sharp claws that will tear you apart and devour you if you look at it too long, which is about thirty seconds, or long enough to get caught staring. That's what love is.

It's that simple. See, the reason it felt like my insides were being ripped out—now get this—was because they *were* being ripped out. Sometimes things are so obvious we don't see them. Maybe we don't want to see them. Like breathing, for instance. I don't notice myself breathing except when I can't, which only happens under two conditions: when I am underwater and when I'm around Laura. If I am ever underwater *with* Laura, it'll be the end of me.

Remember when I said that she might be cruel and I would write about it later? Well, it's later and she's definitely cruel, so I'm writing about it. How cruel? Let's just say it all comes down to the fact that she's playing me like those dueling banjos in *Deliverance*. She gets some kind of joy out of this on-again/off-again thing because she's a Fedora and they get their jollies tormenting each other. So doing it to me is no big deal. I just happen to be some kid she goes to school with. So she presses her breasts into me and gets me all worked up only to brush me off later and tell me I'm a smartass cause I don't know who Earl Scheib is. Well, I don't know and I don't care. Then she makes fun of me and where I live, which she had to see because she's so damn nosy. To top it off, she tells me to drop dead if I don't play along with her little game and make fun of myself. Well, I'm not going to drop dead. In fact, she can drop dead for all I care, because she's caused me nothing but grief ever since I met her, and there's nothing romantic about that. Nothing at all.

So here are the facts. A good reporter does that: investigates the facts, collects as much data as possible, and then sorts through it looking for clues so he can figure out what's going on. Sometimes he has to step back to do that, which in my case means spending time apart from Laura (not a problem, as I have reported) and realizing that I am in love, which right off the bat makes everything I think, feel, and see suspect. That's Fact One: I am in love—whatever that means—so I can't be trusted with anything, which is going to complicate things. Fact Two: Laura is cruel because of her genetic makeup and upbringing, which I have also reported, so that means she can't be trusted, either. That makes two of us. Beautiful. Fact

Three: I am the Merk and I joke around a lot. I can't help it. People say they can't tell the difference between me joking and me being serious, which I guess could be a problem when I get older, but joking is as much a part of me as cruelty is part of her. Fact Four: I should try to keep my home life and my Fedora life as far apart as possible. It'll be tricky, what with Laura being nosy and mom wanting me to take Kornél everywhere, but I'll just have to figure it out. Fact Five: If something doesn't happen with Laura soon, or at least by the time football camp starts in August, I'm going to throw myself under a bus. Maybe I should tell her that, because at the rate we're going, absolutely nothing will happen. I'll be in even worse shape than I am in now.

As far as techniques go in that department, it's pretty sleazy, I know, but I hear it worked for Carl Johnson, who told his girlfriend, Melissa Quinn, that he suffered from a medical condition known as "dreaded semen backup," DSB for short, and that he would have to be hospitalized if she didn't lend him a hand, so to speak. She did, apparently, and Carl avoided a near death experience. If I have to, I'm not above doing something like that with Laura. Let it be known that I was never an altar boy, despite mom's insistence, although it'll take some practice saying "DSB" with a straight face.[8] Kinda like shopping at Pantry Pride.

Wednesday, July 21
Love Calling

More of the same—waiting and not hearing from Laura Fedora, whom (acc.) I'm now calling Laura Sorta, since we're sorta

---

8 *Mom also wanted to send me to Iggie Prep (see Footnote 7) instead of St. Rita's, which is Augustinian and one of the few coed schools around (maybe the only one). I talked her out of it using the $$$$ argument, as in St. Rita's cost less and offered me more. It was still a close call. If she had sent me there, I wouldn't have met Laura and none of this would be happening right now, which is messing with my head.*

together and sorta not. Who knows, really? Then there's camp, which is filled with bicycle pumps and pig shit and little kids having to go to the bathroom all the time. So at the last counselors' meeting I said we should stop giving them water and fruit juice, but all the girls got irate and yelled at me. Anyway, I've been thinking about Laura nonstop like the Concorde to Paris and wondering what's going on. Maybe she's been working with Big Butt or outlining our article or just talking on the phone till her jaw drops off. That's when I thought of calling her again, except I couldn't do it from my house, so Tommy said come over to his place cause the Olympics started and we can watch boxing. Also, he has color TV and a phone in the basement. So after work we went over to his house and got everything set up. His mom even made us grilled-cheese sandwiches with sweet pickles. But as soon as we turned the TV on, my mom called all upset about some American Legion guys who died at the Bellevue-Stratford Hotel. I told her we were nowhere near the Bellevue-Stratford and, besides, we weren't in the American Legion.

"Okay, but stay away from the air conditioning from now on," she said.

"Air conditioning?"

"Yes."

"But we're in the basement. They don't even have it on down here."

"Good."

"Why air conditioners?"

"Just stay away from them."

"All of them?"

"Yes, all of them, wise guy. You wanna die?"

She paused, waiting for an answer.

"No."

"All right, then."

After she hung up, I thought about it and decided that I definitely do not want to die, not from air conditioners or anything else. The irony is that Laura is killing me (and not softly with her song, either). So why am I letting it happen? Why let this girl take over my life and move into my head? What's all that about?

"Maybe you should tell her," Tommy said.

"Tell her what?"

"You know, how you feel. Girls like that stuff."

"I don't know how I feel."

"That's even better."

"I wouldn't know what to say."

"I've got just the thing," he said. "You got her number?"

"Sorta."

"Then call her up and play this."

He pulled out a Seals and Crofts album and played "Get Closer," which went something like, *Darlin, if you want me to be closer to you, get closer to me,* which sounded about right, but I told him I wasn't sure.

"Why not?"

"It's kinda lame."

"Whaddya mean lame? It's number eighteen on Casey Kasem. Besides, girls love that stuff. They're all like chocolate covered cherries: hard on the outside but gooey on the inside. Trust me, I know what I'm talking about."

"But Laura's different," I told him.

"Sure she is."

"No, really, she's not a chocolate covered cherry."

"You want her to stop torturing you?"

"Yeah, but..."

"Then just do it."

Tommy's always been a level-headed guy, not like me, and even though this felt a little strange, I went along with it. The problem, though, was that I forgot her number. So I went through all the permutations. Zero in the middle, three digits on either side, the left side starts with 5 like the fingers of my hand and the right side with 6, which is one more than 5, then one plus one is 2, which is the middle number on the left side, and one up from 2 is 3, which is the middle number on the right side...

"I need a pencil and paper," I told him.

"Top drawer, right."

I went to the desk in the corner and started writing it down but realized after a while there was no way I could remember it all, and I wasn't even sure I got the sequence right.

"Are you telling me you didn't write it down?" Tommy asked, taking his eyes off the TV as soon as the Brim Coffee commercial came on.

"I did."

"Okay."

"I can't."

"Why the hell not?"

"I wrote it on the wall in my bedroom."

He stared at me.

"On the wall map, between—"

"Forget that," he said. "Just call your brother and ask him to read it to you."

I hadn't thought of that, what with this being new territory and all, so I called home. Mom answered, asked which hospital they brought me to, and made me swear not to fall asleep or they'd amputate the wrong leg. She finally calmed down when I told her everything was all right, I just needed to talk to Kornél.

"Who?"

"My brother."

She put the phone down and about a half hour later Kornél came on. He sounded like he'd been sleeping.

"Hello?"

"Kornél, listen. I need you to do something for me."

"Who is this?"

"Richard, your brother."

"Really?"

"Yeah, it's me."

"What do you want?

"That's what I'm trying to tell you."

"Where are you?"

"I'm at Tommy's. I need you to do me a favor."

"What kind of favor?"

"I need you to——"

"You ruined my Silly Putty!"

"Oh, my God, Kornél, I'll buy you two more, I promise. I just need you to do a small favor for me."

"Two?"

"Absolutely. Just do this one thing for me, okay?"

"Okay."

"Now listen. Are you listening?"

"Uh-huh."

"Go upstairs to my room and look on the wall map for a phone number. I wrote it in the big blue Arabian Sea in black pen. It's an important number. Can you do that?"

"Arabian Sea?"

"All right, forget that. You know where Africa is?"

"I guess so."

"Well, go to Africa and look to the right. You'll see a phone number. I want you to write it down and then come back to the phone and tell me."

"Africa?"

"Africa."

"That's the big one, right?"

"Yeah, it's big. It looks like the rock you dug up in the yard last year."

"I remember that rock. It was covered with dirt."

"That's right."

"Brown dirt."

"Right, brown. Now, look for the rock, find the number, write it down, and then come tell me, okay?"

Silence.

"All right, first look for the rock. Then find where I wrote the phone number, then come and tell me."

"Tell you what?"

"The phone number. That's why you have to write it down."

Pause.

"Can you do that?"

"I think so."

"I'll be waiting here," I said.

"Where?"

"On the phone."

By the time I got Laura's number (it took three attempts, because the first time Kornél actually went out to the yard), Tommy had scarfed down two chicken sandwiches and a bottle of Yuengling beer he had snuck out of the refrigerator upstairs. I couldn't get too mad, though, because he grabbed one for me, too. So, we practiced synchronizing dialing with placing the needle on the record, which was tricky cause you've got to get it just right, what with the record turning at 33 1/3 rpm and my heart at about 1100.

"All right, let's boogie," Tommy said, belching.

I dialed the number, by some miracle of miracles Laura answered, and I held the receiver to the turntable just as Tommy set the needle down. The song started playing, got to the second verse, and then I heard "click."

"Don't sweat it," Tommy said. "It's a slow song. Let's do it again."

So we did, except this time Laura didn't even listen to the second verse before hanging up. The third time, it just rang and rang without anyone answering. "I told you she's not a chocolate cherry," I said, relieved.

"What can I say, dude? I guess you were right. So, let's see what's happening with Michael Spinks."

Just as we turned the Olympics back on and I started thinking about kidnapping Laura all over again, the phone rang. We didn't think anything of it till Tommy's mother called from upstairs.

"Tommy, there's a phone call for Richard."

"Okay, we got it, thanks."

"My mother again. Probably another dead Legionnaire," I told him, picking up. Except it wasn't mom. It was Laura.

"What the hell was all that?" she yelled, fuming.

"What?"

"Don't play stupid, Merk. I know it was you cause I dialed star sixty-nine and guess whose number came up?"

"Uh, Tommy's?"

"Uh, yeah. And what the hell were you playing that lame ass song for? God, I knew you were stuffy, but that's ridiculous!"

I stood there holding the receiver.

"Well?"

"I was just trying to say that maybe we could, you know—"

"What, get closer? If you want to get closer, you'll have to work a lot harder than what you've been doing. I never even hear from you. And it'll never happen playing that dumb ass crap. Got me?"

"You never hear from me?" I asked.

"Next time try Aerosmith."

"Are you serious?"

"Is there a better band?"

"No, there'll be a next time?"

"Maybe, maybe not, but guess what? I just heard they're coming to the Spectrum next month."

Pause.

"Aerosmith," she said.

"Got it."

"And, by the way, tell your brother I really liked talking to him. He's a lot nicer than you, you know."

"Yeah, that's what I—"

Click.

Laura's sneaky, I mean really sneaky. Once she found out the prank calls were coming from Lindeman's, she called my house to see if I was home. That's when Kornél told her all about Africa and her phone number on the wall and everything. This confirms that I will never in a million years figure her out. And then I find out she's mad because she hasn't heard from me when all this time I've been complaining about the same thing! So she has her own version of The Great Question like mine—who knew? I guess it's up to me now to make sure we see each other and act like a couple, but I don't see how I can do that when I have to work and look after Kornél all at the same time. I'd have to be Superman. On top of that, I'm supposed to get Aerosmith tickets to prove my undying love for her or something. I bet they're expensive, too. Then again, I can't believe she wants to go with me. I guess we're sorta on again. Sorta.

Saturday, July 24
The Beginning of All Things Amazing

An amazing thing happened to me today. Actually, two amazing things happened, both connected to each other in a way that, if I play my cards right, will lead to an out-of-this-world experience for the record books. I'll be an Olympic champion like Bruce Jenner. I have to write it down, though, because it's completely crazy. I never would have dreamt it, let alone thought about doing it. And it all came from none other than dad—Dad!—as in my Old Man. I never would have thought that, either. I hardly talk to him. I've said that before but I'm saying it again, because it's true even though most people don't believe it, like Mrs. Fedora. His English is really good, not like mom's, except for a strange upturn of his voice at the end of sentences, which must come from those cold Budapest winters I've heard so much about.[9] Maybe it's from drinking goat milk.

---

9 Dad has this joke where he says, "You know, it was cold in Budapest yesterday." You're supposed to ask, "How cold was it?" Then he puts his thumb up between his forefinger and middle finger and says, "This cold!"

So, this morning I was sitting at the kitchen table trying to figure out how to buy the Aerosmith tickets and spend more time with the object of my desire, which will mean less time at home, the object of my un-desire, when dad walked in all shaved and dressed for the day. That's Amazing Thing #1, because I can't remember the last time he did that. He fixed himself a bowl of wheat germ with honey and started talking to me about airport runways and this project he'd been working on—a variable—that "will make the length of tarmac that planes use for take-off and landing count for something." In that way, it was more than a variable, it was a Great Equalizer, making all measured distance the same. It didn't matter if it was a mile of rarified stratosphere at 35,000 feet or just some lowly strip of hot, scuffed-up asphalt on the runway. It would still count for something. See, what he was working on wasn't just a mathematical formula for "stoop-shouldered engineers." It was a Mercurius Variable for the Downtrodden and Oppressed. It was the Variable of Democracy. Even so, it would take time for people to understand its full significance. Something like that.

"It sounds terrific, like the Statue of Liberty," I said.

"Yes, it's another chance for the huddled masses to breathe free."

"So, what is it a variable of?"

"Distance."

"Distance?"

"Distance."

Here, he leaned forward and, with a hint of English Leather on his face, said in a serious voice, "For calculating frequent flyer miles, but I can't tell you the details just yet. I should be done by the end of summer. Last night was a breakthrough, though. I'm telling you, Richard, if everything goes according to Hoyle, we'll be filthy rich. I've always liked that expression, 'filthy rich.' It has a certain ring to it. Don't you agree?"

I nodded, not sure what any of it meant or who Hoyle was, but I definitely liked the idea of being rich. I could go down to Big Al's lot and pay cash for a brand new, 4-speed, 455 Trans Am! Then we'd see just how tough Bobby Fiore really was. It'd also make a big impression on the Fedoras. And Laura, being a Fedora, would bestow some of her figgy graces on me in the garage. The Garage of Figgy Desire. Park your Trans Am in Lot 69 and keep the engine purring.

"So, what are you up to?" he asked.

"Me? Not much, but I think I'm more like the asphalt than rarified air."

"You're feeling downtrodden, Richard?"

"I guess so."

"How so?"

I hadn't seen mom yet, and Kornél was still upstairs in the bathroom, so I figured it was safe. Besides, I actually liked talking to him, so I went for it.

"There's this girl," I said.

"Girl?"

He made it sound like the weirdest thing in the world, like we were a family of frogs or something and what was I doing with a human.

"Her name's Laura."

"Let me stop you right there. You know that women are a lot more complex than aerodynamics or mathematical formulae, right?

"Sure, dad, but—"

"And much more dangerous."

"Yeah, but—"

"If anybody ever invented an algorithm to figure them out, he'd be a millionaire and maybe get elected president."

I wasn't too sure what an algorithm was, but I figured he was trying to tell me something. "Millionaire" reminded me of "Legionnaire," which reminded me of mom, who wasn't exactly a woman but who seemed pretty straightforward. All you had to do was not piss her off. I knew that much, but apparently dad didn't, not for all of his variables and formulae, because he kept pissing her off all the time. Of course, it made sense that Laura was more complex than algorithms. Even dad could tell that.

"Tell me about her," he said.

"Really?"

"I want to hear everything."

"Okay. She's kinda nice but sometimes not. She can be pretty mean, but sometimes she's all right. She changes her mind a lot and then gets ideas mid-sentence and takes off and you have no idea what's going on or where she's headed. Usually, though, I go along, like racing in the heat to the walnut tree at Valley Forge on the Fourth of July. But I still don't know if she likes me or not. I think she does and sometimes she acts like it, but then other times she acts like she can't stand me. She's beautiful, too, with bright red hair and hazel eyes and the most perfect feet you've ever seen. Her toes are slender but not too thin or bony and her instep is as smooth as pumpkin pie. Most of the time she paints her toenails, which are really amazing. When we first met they were pink and she wore sandals and kept pumping her foot back and forth with all these other people in the room and my throat started to get tight. It was the first time I saw her and I'll never forget it for as long as I live."

I looked up to see him staring at me. The munching of wheat germ had stopped. I guess I got carried away. I couldn't believe I was talking to my dad about Laura.

"Pumpkin pie?" he asked.

"She reminds me of Thanksgiving."

"Maybe you're thankful you met her."

"I think about her a lot."

"How did you meet?"

"At school. We're on the paper."

"She's a writer, too?"

"A journalist. She wants to be like some woman reporter who shot herself on television."

"Sounds intense."

"That's Laura. I don't think she'll shoot herself, but she might shoot me one of these days. Or her father will. They're kinda hotheaded people and not the nicest. She's already knocked me down, lied to me, yelled at me for calling her, then yelled at me for not calling her. She says I should pay more attention to her and do things like invite her over, but every time I get close she pushes me away. Oh, and she says I'm stuffy, *stuffy*. What do you call that?"

"Love."

"Really?"

"Maybe."

"Maybe?"

"Give me a minute."

He got a serious look on his face, and I could tell he was really thinking, because when he gets like that he stares into a corner of the room or up at the ceiling and won't come back down till he's found what he's looking for. It can last a while. I've seen people who have just met him actually look up to see what's stuck to the ceiling.

"Adolescence," he said finally.

"But Laura's really mature. She even takes care of her grandpa, and she told me she'll be working at her father's business in the fall."

"What business?"

"They own Fedora Auto Sales and Transport on South Street."

"I see. So she's a fast woman."

I wasn't sure if it was a joke or not, but he started snickering, which is what he does when he tells a joke that nobody else gets.

"Just one more question," he said.

"What's that?"

"What do you see in a girl who knocks you down, yells at you, acts unstable, and whose role model is someone who committed suicide on television?"

"What are you getting at?"

"Why are you interested in someone who may be crazy?"

"She's the sexiest girl I ever met."

"She may be the craziest."

"Isn't that the same thing?"

"Fine line, Richard, fine line."

"Well, I'm hoping she'll change once we get to know each other. We've had some nice talks already. It's not like she's crazy all the time. She's just different."

"People don't change."

"They don't?"

"I'm afraid not. They may do different things on the outside, but they stay the same on the inside, where it counts. The irony is that everyone wants to be someone else. That's the real American dream, I think, not owning your own home. You see it all the time, even that tennis player, the guy who became a woman and tried to play with the women but they wouldn't let him because of his DNA, and he got disqualified. But the dream wasn't real, because what happens is we don't become someone else as we get older. We can't become someone else. Why would we even want to? The older we get, the more we become who we are, not who we aren't. Look at me. I'm more me now than I've ever been."

I had a hard time following all that but finally said, "You are?"

"Absolutely."

"Is that good?"

"The best."

Now I was really stumped, especially when I thought about the penguins. If what made a penguin a penguin was something on the inside, then what made a tennis player a tennis player was on the inside, too, so it didn't matter if the guy had an operation to become a woman or even if he changed his mind later on and became a man again. Was that even possible (I thought of subtraction and addition)? Anyway, if what made Laura Laura was on the *inside*, then the way she acted on the *outside* didn't matter and could even change. So maybe I was right to believe she would change. Then again, what dad said sounded right, too. Maybe Laura, being a Fedora, would become even nastier by the time she got to college. You know, wear war paint like her mother and breathe fire like her father. If so, then the journalism professor deserved everything he had coming to him and a whole lot more. I wouldn't want to be in his penny loafers. I guess it all came down to what Laura was really like on the *inside*.[10] Dad said she's crazy, which is hard to dispute. I said I'm the one who's crazy—about her—which is also hard to dispute. Truth is, I don't know who's right. What if it turns out we're both right?

"The important thing, Richard, is to be true to the person you really are."

"Who is that?"

"Who is what?"

"The person I really am."

"I don't know."

"You don't?"

"No, but you can reverse engineer it."

"I can?"

"Sure. If your follow your dream, your dream will tell you. See, there are all these unconscious things floating around in your head that are part of the real you. The thing you have to do is shake them up."

"Sounds like a snow globe," I said.

"It's psychology."

"Oh."

"And don't let rejection get you down. Remember what my Uncle Vencel, the great Hungarian astronomer, used to say."

He paused, waiting for me to finish the sentence, which I did. "Per aspera ad astra," I said, and only then did I realize that

---

10 *I'll have to think about this whole inner/outer thing, since it keeps coming up and is probably more of a big deal than I know. Seriously, how can they not be connected? If I think about what I said before—a woody—then what happens on the outside (the woody) is related to what happens on the inside (love). You can't have one without the other, the woody and love, right? So, maybe there are penguins somewhere that can fly, or maybe they used to fly but got stuck living around a lot of Antarctic water and just forgot how. I'll have to check it out on the map. All I know is, this is giving me a headache.*

Amazing Thing #2 had just happened. It was a sign from God—a confirmation (get it?)—of my plan to kidnap Laura and lie naked with her while eating figs and biscotti. It was the answer to The Great Question and a surefire way for her to see that I am not some Stuff-Pot but one cool dude *á la* Steve McQueen in the chase scene in *Bullet*. It couldn't be any clearer, so I decided to set things in motion right there and then. I'm just that kind of guy. Nothing will get in my way now. Not no way, not no how.

Sunday, July 25
Norm Fay by the Way

I skipped Mass today and hope that I don't run into Fr. Szemeredi anytime soon. I went down to Robin's Books on South 13th, which is this smelly little place on the second floor of an old store or apartment or whatever, because somebody said that that's the place to go for everything and you might even run into a poetry reading or a meeting of the Philadelphia Socialists or something like that. I didn't see any socialists, not that I'd know what they look like except maybe for long hair, but I did think of a group with an awesome acronym: the Pen & Ink Society—PENIS for short (or long). They could be writers like me looking for a little Figgy Love, except I'm serious about the kidnapping plan, because I believe it will show Laura once and for all that I am a force to be reckoned with. I figure kidnapping will pretty much do it.

So I started looking in their "Travel USA" section for a place to go where we would be left alone but could still go to school and get jobs like at the local car dealership. See, the way I figure it, she could get a job as a bookkeeper's assistant or something like that, and I could sell cars, pretty much be the button-down kid from back East you can trust with helping you find the Right Car at the Right Price at the Right Time and not get screwed over like at Fedora Auto Sales Where They Pull a FAST One (could be a jingle). How hard could it be, really? I could *parlez-vous* with customers on vacation from Paris or Haiti. That would be a huge plus for the dealership, and if they wanted to have a promotional deal like Toga Sunday, I could dress in a Roman senatorial toga and quote Tacitus to the customers. It'd be a riot and make the dealership a ton of money. Come on, who wouldn't go for that? Big Al should try it. He could have the salesmen wear togas with their fedoras. It'd probably make the news. But then I was talking to this guy, some clerk at the store, who said that if I wanted a job at a car dealership, why was I looking in the travel section?

"I dunno."

"Well, how old are you, anyway?"

"Fifteen and a half."

"A half?"

"Five months."

"So how are you going to work at a dealership?"

"My girlfriend's dad owns one."

"I see."

I get that a lot, "I see." The guy was older with a scruffy beard and scraggily hair and black Army glasses. He wore a Philadelphia Broad Street Bullies t-shirt from 1973 and red running shoes. There was only one other person in the bookstore, so I guess he was bored, figured he'd help the kid out.

"So, you're taking a vacation?" he asked.

"Well, yeah, except I don't know where yet. That's why I wanted to check out the travel books."

"Driving?"

"Definitely."

"So you have a car?"

"Not yet."

"But you're getting one from your girlfriend's father?"

"Sorta, yeah."

"And you have a license?"

"Kinda."

He stared at me.

"My girlfriend's driving. She has the license," I explained. "I have a permit, so when she gets tired I can drive."

He rubbed his jaw and said, "Sounds like a pretty good plan, except for one little detail."

"What's that?"

"They're only good in state. If you cross the state line with a learner's permit and get stopped, they'll ticket both of you and make her drive the rest of the way."

"Oh. I guess I never thought of that."

He nodded and started walking away but then hurried back like he dropped his wallet.

"Let me see if I have this right. You're looking for a place to drive to with your girlfriend in her father's car?"

I nodded slowly.

"And does her father know you're taking his car?"

"Not exactly."

"So, you're running away," he said, grinning.

"No!"

"Sure you are."

You never know how hot it can get on the second floor of a bookstore in Philadelphia in July until you're actually standing there. The guy was blocking the stairs and the rancid smell of used books was making me sick.

"Don't sweat it. I was fifteen once. I know what you're going through. So, tell me, is she pretty?"

I nodded again.

"Good, cause if you're running away with the girl, she'd better be worth it. Is she your age, too?"

"Older."

"But she's not eighteen?"

"No."

"That makes it easier. At least you're both under age, so maybe you won't be charged with kidnapping."

I choked.

"Where do you want to go?" he asked.

"I dunno."

"Well, how far does it have to be? Jersey? New York? Montreal? For chrissakes, I hope not Montreal. I hate the Canadiens."

I thought for a minute and, wanting to get as far away from the Fedoras as possible, said "Wyoming." Actually, there was a picture book about Wyoming on the shelf just above his head.

"Is that so?"

"Yeah, Wyoming. We talked about it, and we both like buffaloes and tepees and stuff like that."

"Buffaloes?"

"And tepees."

"Well, you're in luck, Tepee Man. It just so happens that's where I'm from."

"No way."

"Yep, grew up in Cheyenne. That's where Interstate Eighty passes through the southern part of the state. A lot of Easterners take it on their way to California and such. Three thousand miles from New York to San Francisco."

He actually said, "and such."

"Is that the one they made the song about?"

"No, that's Route Sixty-Six: two thousand miles from Chicago to LA. But here's the funny part. When I was your age, I got a job working for the US Forest Service in Cody. I was a spotter for forest fires. It was one of the best jobs I ever had. Made like a dollar a day and got to live in a tree house."

"Really?"

"No lie. So maybe instead of selling cars or whatever they'll have you doing—and, no offense, but you'll probably end up washing them—why not work for the Forest Service?"

"I do like the smell of pine," I said. "Do they have pine trees there?"

"Son, how the hell do you think they made tepees back in the day? Lodgepole pine."

"Then I'll do it."

"Great, and I'll help you." Then, sticking out his hand, he said, "The name's Norm by the way, Norm Fay."

"Nice to meet you Norm Fay. I'm Richard, but my friends call me Merk."

"Merk?"

"My last name's Mercurius."

"You mean like the car?"

"No, it's Hungarian."

"Is that so? My second wife was Hungarian. Nastiest hellcat you ever met."

"I'm sorry."

"Don't be. She died in a copper mine accident in Chile, but that's another story. Let's get you a road map to Wyoming and a trip planner. So, you two stayin in hotels, motels, rest stops, all night diners, what?"

I hadn't thought about that and wondered what Laura would say if we pulled up to a dive with blinking neon lights that said Shady Pines Motel and Diner, Open 24 Hours. But that might pale compared to what she would do when she found out I was kidnapping her. There was obviously a lot to consider here.

"To tell you the truth, we haven't gotten that far yet."

"Still on first base? That's all right, kid. You just pack some condoms, a sleeping bag, and a flask and you'll be fine."

"But there's more to it," I told him.

"More?"

"I mean other stuff."

He waited.

"The thing is..."

My legs started wobbling and my mouth got as dry as cotton, or maybe a Wyoming cactus. I wasn't even sure they had cactus in Wyoming. I knew they didn't have cotton. And what was the plural of cactus—cactus, cactuses, cacti? Who says "cacti," really? But even before thinking about flora, I had to wonder what in God's name I was doing talking to this guy, a perfect stranger. I wasn't afraid he'd turn me in or anything like that, not when he just told me to buy rubbers and have sex with an underage girl, but it was still embarrassing. I've learned that when you're planning a kidnapping, you have to be very careful who you tell. One slip-up and it's over. Up till now I hadn't told anyone. I wasn't sure talking to Norm was the right thing to do.

"Are there cactuses in Wyoming?" I asked.

"What?"

"What I mean is...do you think...I could have a glass of water?"

Norm hurried off, came back with a glass of ice water, pulled up a three-legged stool, and had me sit on it.

"First, drink the water," he said.

I drank, ice cubes clunking in the pink plastic cup.

"Now, tell me what's going on."

"All right, here's the thing. I'm scared," I told him.

"Of what?"

"Kidnapping Laura."

"Who's Laura?"

"My girlfriend, except it's not official yet, so I don't even know if she *is* my girlfriend."

"What's not official?"

"Us going together. It's not like it's public where everybody knows we're boyfriend and girlfriend, which is why I have to kidnap her."

"You're kidnapping her to make it official?"

"When you put it that way it sounds weird, but that's right."

"Then maybe you shouldn't do it," he said. "I have to tell you it sounds a little extreme. How do you know she won't like you without the kidnapping?"

"Because I've tried everything and so far nothing's worked. I even called her up and played Seals and Crofts, which is why I'm worried that if I don't make a dramatic statement like kidnapping her, things will just stay the same or get worse."

"Seals and Crofts?"

"I got bad advice."

"And what makes you think you need a 'dramatic statement?' What if you just told her how you feel? Isn't that dramatic enough?"

"That's what Tommy said."

"Who's Tommy?"

"My best friend."

"Well, maybe he's right. I don't see why you would kidnap a girl just cause she might not like you. And who says kidnapping her is going to make her like you? That doesn't make a whole lotta sense, I gotta tell you."

"So if I had a reason that made sense, then it would be all right?"

"I dunno. I flunked Moral Philosophy in grad school—got caught cheatin—but I can tell you one thing. You'll need something more than Seals and Crofts if you're gonna pull this off."

"That's just what Laura said."

I had to think about this, because Norm was the first—and so far only—person to hear about the plot. Oh, my God, it was now a plot! I had actually hatched a plot like it was an egg or something! And not a robin's egg, even though I was in Robin's Bookstore, but an alligator egg: a huge, speckled alligator egg (again, *Wild Kingdom*). I got that sick feeling again, but then I remembered the whole reason I was there, the original *raison d'être*. That must have been *raison d'énough*. Keep your eye on the ball, Merk!

"Look, if I kidnap her it'll show how serious I am and we'll finally get to spend time together. Besides, it's not like I'm a real kidnapper or anything like that."

"You're not going to tie her up?"

"No!"

"And you won't hurt her or go crazy?"

"No, of course not. I just want my Great Question answered, that's all."

"What's your great question?"

"Why is Laura never around when I need her, and why does she act like I'm the last thing in the world she thinks about?"

"That's two questions."

"Well, you know what I mean."

"And that's it?"

"That's enough, isn't it? It's driving me crazy. I can't stop thinking about it—and her feet."

"Her feet?"

"They're beautiful, Norm."

"Well, I don't know about feet, but there sure are plenty of things that drive me crazy," he said, shaking his head and staring at the indoor-outdoor carpeting, which had huge stains and was ripped from foot traffic.

"All right," he said. "If you do this thing, kidnap Laura and drive off to Wyoming, the two of you will fall in love and live happily ever after while looking out for forest fires as you sit naked in a tree house, which will become your lodgepole love shack. At night you'll sleep in the cold mountain air covered in buffalo hide and holding each other so tight your hearts will beat as one. Is that the plan?"

"Finally, somebody gets it!"

"Sure I do."

"Does it sound crazy?"

"Only if it doesn't work or her family presses charges. That's how history judges these things, you know. They're crazy only if they fall flat on their face. Otherwise, you're a hero. And you're already a hero in my book, kid, even with the foot fetish, which is a little strange, although I've heard worse."

"Why?"

"Not many people are into feet, I guess."

"No, why am I a hero?"

"Because you had the balls to come up with the idea in the first place. Hardly anybody gets that far, let alone pulls it off."

"Thanks, Norm."

"Don't mention it. But are you sure it'll work? I mean that you'll even get out of Pennsylvania? I'm a little doubtful on that score."

"Oh, it'll work, trust me."

"How do you know?"

"I've got confirmation."

"Really, from who?"

At this point I felt comfortable enough with Norm-by-the-Way to venture a little grammatical correction.

"*Whom.*"

"Really?"

"I'm a purist."

"All right, whom."

I crunched some ice, swallowed, and said softly, "God."

That, combined with the foot thing and grammatical correction, should have been enough to get me thrown out of the store. I thought about Big Al sending me flying through the screen door on South Adriana, which would have been what the "F" stood for. But, thankfully, Norm was not Big Al and was nice enough not to tell me I was crazy. He even spent the next two hours helping me plan out a route—not on Interstate 80 or 70, cause "that's exactly where they'll be lookin for you"—but on a bunch of smaller highways and roads that looked like the bullfrog we dissected in Biology and included 1 South to Maryland; 340 West to Virginia; 50 West through West Virginia, Ohio, and Indiana; 52 West through Indiana; 36 West to Illinois (where we would pass our fourth "Jefferson Davis Highway," which I thought was strange); 24 West to Missouri; 83 North to Nebraska, which would take us to 6 West to Colorado; and, finally, 85 North to Cheyenne. All in all, a trip of about 25,000 miles by the look of it on the map.

"Here's the name and number of an Army buddy. He owns a body shop in Cheyenne. When you get there, give him a call and he'll help you out."

"Thanks, Norm. I appreciate it. How long do you think it'll take?"

"That all depends."

"On what?"

"How fast you drive. That's the variable in all this. Distance is a constant. Speed, that's your variable."

"Speed?"

"Speed."

This had to be Amazing Thing #3, because yesterday it was Distance and now it was Speed. What was next? It had to be Time, right? Sure it was. I learned that from Fr. Leopold Kreps, an Augustinian friar and astrophysicist from the Vatican who gave a lecture at St. Rita's last year on "retrocausality," which at first I thought had to do with wearing skinny ties but then found out different. It was in the auditorium and everybody had to go. I think it was last year. It could have been next year.

"How can I thank you, Norm?"

"Two ways: one, don't get caught and, two, don't get caught."

"Anything else?"

"Send me a postcard with a buffalo on it. Can you do that?"

"Sure."

"When do you leave?"

"Laura wants to go to this concert August thirteenth at the Spectrum, so I'm planning on doing it that night on the way home, except it won't be on the way home. It'll be on the way to Wyoming, which I think is a song."

Norm didn't laugh. He looked at me through his glasses, adjusted them, and didn't say a word.

"What's wrong?"

"August thirteenth?" he asked.

"Yeah."

"That's Friday the thirteenth."

"No, it isn't."

"Sure it is," he said, pointing to a Bicentennial wall calendar behind him.

This happens to me all the time. It's like a Mercurius curse or something. If dad has a Mercurius Variable, I've got a Mercurius Curse. It's not fair, but there it is. Just when I think I've gotten ahead, made progress, or figured something out, this happens. It's like I can never win, never get to where I'm headed without some monkey wrench being thrown in from out of the blue, pardon the mixed metaphors, but it drives me up the wall. Kind of like Odysseus trying to find his way home and getting sidetracked by all kinds of things: storms, goddesses, sirens, a cyclops, you name it. But, honestly, it was too late. I was committed. I had the books, the maps, and the plan. All I needed were the Aerosmith tickets, and there was no other concert date in Philly. This was it, do or die. Besides, God was with me. What could go wrong, right?

"I gotta go, Norm."

"I understand."

I paid $11.59 for everything, including the Wyoming picture book (he gave me his 15% employee discount), and started down the stairs to the street. I had just spent nearly three hours in Robin's Books and was exhausted. I turned around at the bottom for one last look—because in addition to being obsessive, I'm sentimental (or mental)—and there was Norm standing at the top of the stairs, watching me. His red running shoes stuck out past the steps.

"Just send me a postcard," he said, adjusting his glasses again.

"You got it," I told him, "from Yellowstone."

Then I left, the little bell at the top of the door ringing goodbye as if an angel had just gotten its wings.

Tuesday, July 27

I went for a run today after work. I had to. I have to do it to keep sane what with the "plot" and penguins and everything else running through my head. So I have these Nike Waffle Trainers with a yellow stripe that I wear, because my regular running shoes are in my locker at school. And even though they let us keep the lockers through the summer, because Coach said we're supposed to be training all the time, even when we're asleep (I don't think he's too bright), I left them there and never take them home, because I never run anymore or at least I haven't since meeting you know who of the hat family. Now, I spend all my time thinking about her and those feet that I've never kissed and the toes I've never sucked.

There, I said it. I know it's perverted and I can never tell anyone except the priest who's with me when I die. Otherwise, I'll go to hell where, apparently, it's okay to be a toe sucker, not that I think there's anything wrong with it, because I read in a Human Sexuality book that anything between two consenting adults is A-OK. Well, we're not exactly adults, but that's all right, because I'm not even sure I know what consenting means. For instance, I say and do things all the time I don't mean, so if I consent to A and then do B, is that taking my consent back, or did I never give it in the first place? If I go ahead with B, is the consent for A still there? Also, do I actually have to consent to B, or does the paperwork from A cover me? I don't get it, which is why I went for a run. I get the things that happen to me on a run like the pain in my side or my lungs exploding or on a really good day feeling like I'm flying high above the houses in my neighborhood. Anyway, it was time to do a lot of sweating and even more spitting. I love spitting and do a lot of it, which drives Tommy crazy, which is one reason we don't train together. The other is, honestly, he's too slow for me even though he's tall and lanky. I'm sure he can beat me in the water hands down, but when it comes to feet, nobody's better than me, trust me. I don't know why that is, except that I don't eat a lot and am pretty thin. Lately, I haven't been eating at all.

I ran north down 7th from the Edgar Allan Poe house past Moore and York to Lehigh and back again. It wasn't bad except for a stray dog on Jefferson that I had to stop for and the fact that it was all sidewalk and street, which, combined with the Nikes, which are really for the track, probably did me more harm than good. But

I figure why worry about that now? It's not like I'll be competing anymore or gearing up for the fall. And there'll be very little running once we're in our tree house. Or maybe there'll be trails I can run on in the woods. I hadn't thought about that. I love running. How can I give it up? I couldn't wear the Nikes, though, probably tear them to shreds and my feet, too. Maybe there are special trail shoes I can buy. You know, like Eskimo shoes for snow, except these would be for running on pine needles and rocks. I should ask Coach about that. He might know. Wait, are there *Rattle Snakes* there?!?

So, I've been thinking about stuff and wondering what to do and it came to me in one of those *coups* to ask dad for the money to buy the tickets for the concert. Why not? After our talk, he'd probably want to help me out with a little advance from his Variable for the Downtrodden and Oppressed (come on, who could be more deserving?) and not mention a word to mom, who would freak out that I was on drugs or something and having underage sex with oversexed adults. I wish that were true, but it's obviously not. I'd gladly do the time grounded in my room if that ever happened, but no such luck, not yet at least. So, I'll ask dad and I bet he'll give me the money, and then I'll be set. He said we're going to be filthy rich, right? Once I have the tickets, I can go over to Laura's place and we can start hanging out and making plans (and messing around), which should take care of her Great Question. My God, how was I supposed to know she had one and that it was the same as mine? What are the odds of that? It's like a million to one.

I got back from my run and it was a nice day, not too hot, so I sat out front on the porch in the shade of the chestnut tree. I sat there watching people and cars and buses across the empty lot opposite our house on Kingsbury. And then it hit me, another *coup*: I have to get a car.[11] I wasn't serious about stealing one from Big Al's

---

11 *Between the coups and Amazing Things that keep happening, I figure the constellations are aligned just right for pulling this thing off. Dad could probably calculate the exact date of our arrival in Cheyenne on his Stargazer Wheel. I hope he doesn't get the chance.*

lot, even though I saw this movie once and there was a big board in the salesroom where they hung the keys. I happen to know that a lot of times they just keep them above the sun visor in the car. Jimmy Grabowski had a job last summer in the Service Dept. of the local AMC dealership and told me. It'd be a piece of cake. Of course, that'd make me a car thief and the police would come after us. Mom would have a heart attack for sure and be so embarrassed she wouldn't be able to go to Mass anymore or be seen by any of her friends. I don't want to be responsible for that. It's bad enough her one son has problems and the other one imagines sucking girls' toes. She'd die for sure. Then again, why am I worried about stealing a car when I'm kidnapping Laura?

I don't know what's happening to me, really. I never imagined I'd be figuring out ways to kidnap some girl with a stolen car so we could live in a tree house in the Wild Wild West. I mean, it sounds like I'm on acid or something. It made sense to Norm, but now I'm wondering if he's all there. What kind of adult—let's be honest, here—works in a bookstore, wears red running shoes, has been divorced at least twice, and helps teenagers run away from home? No, I shouldn't say that. Norm was cool. He looked at me like I was a little off for a second or two. I caught him. But I guess I deserved it. I'm doing all this for love, that beast with two backs, so maybe I have an excuse and the courts will go easy on me. They'll have to—I'm not prison material—I wouldn't last two days. Laura wouldn't press charges or anything, would she? I'm not a car thief or kidnapper, just some college prep-type guy who studies Latin and wants to do what everybody else is doing but doesn't have any luck at all. Maybe I should stop trying.

I've come up with five possible titles for my novel. I haven't decided on one yet, but I think it's important to start with the title, because it's a name. The name of anything is what gives it its identity and uniqueness (even Kornél knows that). That's why it's important to be careful what you name your kid, cause he could go through life either really lucky or screwed up, especially if he's called something like Moonbeam or Sunrise. Just think of *A Boy Named Sue*. By starting with the title, I figure I can focus each scene and chapter on the plot instead of letting the characters wander around like Israelites in the desert. I've read too many books like that. The title acts like a guide, keeping you on track. So, here are the titles I have so far: *My Life as a Pineapple Upside Down Cake; Inside Out and Upside Down; The Story of a Red Fedora; Love Interrupted; Kidnapping Laura*. I'm not sure about the last one, though, because it will remind people of what I did or am about to do or am premeditating. They give you extra jolts for premeditation, you know. I also don't want the novel to be just about kidnapping, although that would probably sell books and make me a ton of dough that I could use to buy rugs for the tree house and maybe some fishing gear. I'd like to learn fly fishing. But a novel has to be about more than that. It's supposed to tell a story, my story. So what is my story? How can I figure out my story when I don't even know the real me? How does that work?

I sat there for a long time not doing anything, trying to figure out the real me, and the only thing I could think of was running and smelling shoes and doing things with Laura's feet. If that's the real me, I'm in trouble. Other guys are out there going to college and making money and working on the Alaska Pipeline, but I smell shoes. It's more than a little discouraging, but I have to admit I'm more than a little excited about driving thousands of miles with Laura on back roads to Wyoming. There'll probably be lots of places to buy souvenirs and arrowheads and stuff like that. Maybe we'll see some real tepees. That would be great, but I'm starting to feel paralyzed and I don't know why. Maybe I'm about to have a heart attack or something. It's starting to feel like I'm underwater or in Kornél's world. I don't know what that's like exactly, but it can't be good. He's got his own stuff going on and comes in and out of reality to eat and see how everybody's doing. And to nag me about Silly Putty. It started in the bookstore, this feeling, and it's getting worse, creeping up on me like Lindeman. It's like I'm a girl.

Friday, July 30
The Envelope

The next time I see dad might be at graduation (he'll probably come) but I can't wait that long, so I wrote him a note and slipped it under his door Wednesday night. I knocked just to be polite, but I know he never answers. So I put it under his door explaining everything. I was very careful writing it, and it took three drafts before getting it right. Here's draft two, which is pretty close to the final one, which, as I said, I left for him:

Dear Dad,

Thanks for the talk last weekend. I appreciate your help trying to figure things out with me and Laura. But if I want to find out if she's crazy or not, I have to spend time with her, like you and mom. That's logical, right? So, here's the thing. We want to go to this concert in two weeks at the Spectrum. Each ticket costs $6.00, for a total of $12. Rounded out for gas and food (she likes bagels), it's about $20, but I don't have enough money. Could you let me have some, even a little? I'll give you a full report when I get back, I promise. And I'll keep Uncle Vencel's advice in mind as I follow my dream, PER ASPERA AD ASTRA!

Your Son,
Richard

PS—please don't tell mom about this. It's just between us men, okay?

It occurred to me after reading it that his first question would be, "Where is he going to get a car to put the gas in?"

He's detail-oriented like that. Well, with some details like gas and asphalt and variables, but not women. So I have to take everything he says with Two-and-a-Half Grains of Salt. He's not very practical and kind of a nerd. I don't mean to be cruel or anything, but the truth is the truth, and the sooner you own up to it, the better. Otherwise, you could end up really messed up, stare at the ceiling or into empty garbage cans all day. I guess that was a rotten thing to say—there's that louse in me again—but what am I supposed to do? I'm a penguin, lost between swimming and flying, so I waddle around looking for a place to squat for the night.

But then Amazing Thing #4 happened and all of a sudden I'm a Flying Penguin. Forget pigs. When you want to do the impossible, think of penguins flying. I know that's not what people usually think of, but that's me. Amazing Thing #4 happened when I got up this morning to pee and wash my face. I stepped on an envelope under my door that had a neatly ironed twenty-dollar bill inside. I know it was ironed, because I could smell the starch. Dad loves to iron. He says it calms him down (from what I don't know). I guess he decided to give me a fully starched bill for the concert. I'll have to be careful that when I break it, it doesn't split into pieces.[12]

Anyway, the first thing I did after work was go down to the Spectrum and buy the tickets, which was a good thing, because if I had waited any longer, they would have been sold out. By the time I got back home dinner was already on the table, so I put the tickets in the shoebox with my baseball cards, wrapped a red rubber band around the box, washed up, and flew downstairs to supper. Mom brought up the Legionnaires again and how 23 of them died so far from bad air conditioning and that it was a blessing in disguise that we could never afford air conditioning and that God was protecting us. We should each (me and Kornél) get down on our faces and pray in thanksgiving for HIS protection and the presence of our Guardian Angels.

---

12 *That's a joke.*

"Richard, don't smirk."

"I'm not smirking."

"Don't they teach you anything at Saint Rita's?"

"Sure they do."

"What, how to flirt with girls?"

"That's senior year."

"Don't be a wisenheimer, because the danger is not over."

I looked at her. She was really worried, so I wasn't going to make it worse by asking how we were supposed to get down on our faces.

"What do you mean?" I asked.

"These things come in threes."

"What does?"

"Death, one right after the other."

"I don't get it."

"Death will strike twice more before he's done."

I looked at Kornél and worked my fingers slowly up his arm like a tarantula. I couldn't help it. Then I started howling like a ghost and he laughed.

"Go ahead, make fun, but it always happens that way. It's not over."

"Like all those people in China who died from the earthquake?"

"That was awful, but this is closer to home. It will happen two more times."

I got a serious look on my face, pretended to choke on something, and then went into a spastic fit, throwing myself on the floor.

"That's number two!" Kornél yelled, pointing and laughing.

"Funny guy you are, both of you, but you don't understand how serious this is. Do you see what it did to those poor Legions? The air conditioning is bad, bad to breathe and bad to be around, especially for the young people. Just make sure you stay away from it."

"Sure thing," I said, getting up and dusting myself off.

I decided later that night while Kornél was in my room playing with GI Joe and making a ton of noise that I really would stay away from air conditioning until they know more about what happened to the "Legions" and whether it was mold or dust or just hanging out in an old hotel that killed them. Personally, I think it was the hotel. I've gone by it a million times, cause it's just on the other side of City Hall, and it looks like a fortress or this massive castle. Probably has vampires and extraterrestrial creatures hanging upside down in the closets. But I'll stay away from the air conditioning, anyway, just in case. If mom is right, then I won't get Legionnaire's Disease, but if the whole thing is a bunch of hot, steaming you-know-what, the worst that can happen is I'll sweat a lot, which girls like even though they say they don't. It's part of my insurance policy to stay alive so I can enjoy the fruits of my kidnapping plot, which is starting to come together, believe it or not. I don't believe it myself.

Saturday, July 31
The Dream

Just when things were starting to fall into place, I had to go and have this dream. It wasn't just any dream. It was awful. I dreamt I was flying above the houses on Kingsbury and all around the neighborhood and even dropped a turd on Big Al's dealership (hard and dry), but it ricocheted off the hood of a car and went bouncing down the street without exploding. Big Al

stood there smoking a cigar and laughing at me. Then he jumped up, trying to grab me, but I was too quick and he was too short, so I got away. There I was flying around in my Nikes when all of a sudden I looked down and saw that I was naked. To tell you the truth, I loved it. I highly recommend flying naked to anyone who gets the chance, even if it's just in a dream. I wanted to find Laura and take her away with me, but I wasn't sure I could handle the extra weight, so I did some calculations on a slide rule that I had stuffed into one of my shoes. When I tucked it back in, though, it threw me off balance and I went veering in different directions. There was also the problem of being naked, which would have been fine (I'm an exhibitionist when it comes to naked flesh), except this wasn't how I wanted Laura to see me. Besides, it was starting to get cold in the stratosphere and I was looking a little like dad's joke, which was even more embarrassing than getting a haircut and made me think that looking for Laura wasn't such a great idea after all.

I flew around, anyway, dropping turds here and there and wreaking havoc on the populace below. One of my bombs went straight down the chimney of the Edgar Allan Poe house. It shouldn't have taken them too long to figure out it wasn't a raven's turd.[13] When I got bored, I flew to South Adriana and saw the fig tree in Laura's backyard. Laura was sitting under it, and so I swooped down to see what she was doing. I was expecting the worst, like her being there with some other guy, but when I got closer I could see her sitting alone at a small wooden table with a typewriter working on our article about the ballpark and Earl Sheib. A small glass of grappa sat next to the typewriter, and she took a swig every once in a while. Next to the grappa was a .38 caliber revolver, just in case there were television cameras around, I guess. I landed and told her that I loved her in a psychological way and wanted to marry her.

---

13 *If I owned a bar, I'd call it "The Raven's Turd" and put a picture of Edgar Allan Poe up. See my drawing. I'm thinking of sending it to the museum.*

"You want to marry me?"

"Yes."

"Have you thought this through?"

"It's all I think about."

"I thought you wanted to kidnap me and take me to your tree house in Montana."

"Wyoming."

"Is that true?"

"Kind of."

"Merk, how could you do that?"

"I told you. I love you."

"So you're going to take me away from everything?"

"No, it's not like that."

"What's it like, then?"

"I want us to be together, that's all."

She looked me over from head to Nike. I was nervous, standing there naked, but she didn't laugh or make fun or anything like that. She just stared. It reminded me of the first time we met in Mr. Andrade's office. My right wing twitched a bit.

"I can't," she said finally.

"Why not?"

"I haven't finished the article."

"You can do it when we get to Cheyenne. I'll write it with you. Maybe we can even write it on the road."

"I still can't."

I looked at her.

"It's nonno."

"What about him?"

"He's going to die."

"He's not going to die. He's fine."

"Really? Look at him."

I looked under the tree and saw nonno lying against the trunk, his face ashen and the tips of his eyelids puffy and red. His fedora lay nearby, crushed. Funny, I hadn't noticed him before.

"You see?" she said.

"He's just resting. Maybe he hasn't had his eggs and toast yet."

"You're being a smartass again."

"Forget what I said. Come with me."

"No."

"Yes."

"If I leave him, he'll die. Do you want that on your conscience?"

I shook my head.

"Then don't go to Wyoming. Stay here with me."

"I can't," I said.

"Why not?"

"Cause if he dies, it'll be number two."

She looked at me. "Caca?"

"No, the second death. It'll be horrible, but even more horrible will be what happens after that."

"What's that?"

"Number three."

"What are you talking about?"

"A third person will die."

"Don't talk like that," she said.

"Why? Are you afraid it'll be me?"

"Maybe."

"So you don't want me to die?"

"No."

"Why not?"

"Don't be stupid."

"You love me, don't you?"

"Nope," she said, blowing a bubble.

"How can you chew gum and drink grappa at the same time?" I asked.

"How can you be so smart and still be an ass?"

"Practice."

She grunted.

"I know you love me. It's obvious," I said.

"You that sure of yourself?"

"Yeah, cause you wouldn't have done that chest thing with me under this tree if you didn't love me with all your heart from the bowels of your soul."

She rolled her eyes.

"What about the walnut tree, then?"

"That was an experiment."

"What were you testing?"

"Distance."

"Distance?"

"Distance."

"I don't get it."

"I wanted to see if you could go the distance," she said.

"And?"

"Jury's still out."

"You're killing me, you know that?"

"Softly with my song?"

"No, like Christine Chubbuck."

"Perfect," she said. "You'll be an inspiration to women everywhere."

Without missing a beat, she picked up the .38, pointed it straight at my heart, and pulled the trigger. Blood splattered all over my pearl-colored wings. She sat down to watch me bleed, taking another swig of grappa. Then she put her feet up on the table and smiled. With all the commotion, Big Al came running out to see what was going on, but I flew above the telephone poles and rooftops all the way to the mountains of Wyoming, leaving a trail of blood and tears in the snow. I closed my eyes and flew as high and fast as I could, the smell of balsam filling the air, which was even colder than before, like ice. I didn't care, though, because I was dead, struck down by the girl of my dreams in the prime of my life (just like a number!).

"I'll be damned if she gets the Aerosmith tickets now!" I yelled, shaking my fist in the air and holding my bleeding heart.

Sunday, August I

I'm still shaken up and have to admit that that dream wasn't a good omen at all. Now I'm really scared. I don't know what's going on, what I should do, or what all those confirmations from God meant if this is going to end up with my being shot through the heart not with Cupid's arrow but a slug from Laura's .38. Okay, maybe it won't be by her (I'm still not ruling it out), but maybe by the police when they corner us in Jackson Hole. "Come out of the hole with your hands up! We have your mother with us!" But I'm too young to die. And I have another confession: I haven't been on a real date with anyone, not once. My cousin Aniko doesn't count. That was just for the Hungarian Scouts ball, and the guys kept making fun of me for bringing my sister. I told them to shut the f*cked up. My God, it's the Mercurius Curse all over again!

So I spent most of the day yesterday going over the reasons for kidnapping Laura. I had to talk myself into not returning the twenty bucks to dad and forgetting the Trigger-Happy-Red-Headed-Devil-With-the-Painted-Toes forever. I sat down and wrote it all out as logically as possible, being a writer and all.

The Reasons

1. Kidnapping Laura answers The Great Question, which is becoming more like a Great Pain-in-the-Neck, since I'm starting not to care anymore if she pays attention to me or not. I'm still not getting anything out of this boyfriend/girlfriend thing unless you count the minutes/hours/days/nights/weeks of aggravation. Can I turn those in like Green Stamps? I'll have to check with mom. Maybe if I throw in Clyde Bowden's racket.

2. I'll have a chance to get out of my crummy house, away from my crazy family, out on the road with Laura,

and as far away as possible from my stupid job, which should be paying me $13/hr, never mind $3. What's wrong with that? A guy's got to get out and do things, otherwise he sits at home and rots like a potato, grows tubers even. I guess that's why I like to run and am on the track team. That's probably why I dream about flying, too. I've got to get away for good. Movement is good. It's all about change.

3. Kornél. He's Reason #3, because he'll finally get what he wants, which is to be treated like a normal kid and not a baby. With me gone he won't be stuck at home, because he'll have to take over the Big Brother job and do things like get a job and help with groceries and argue with the electric company about kilowatts and all that stuff. And he can do all the painting he wants. I'll even write a letter to Mr. Andrade and recommend him for a counselor job at the Day Camp. He doesn't know Shakespeare the way I do, but Mr. Andrade can teach him. And, all right, I'll miss him probably, but we'll get over that in a hurry. I can send him postcards whenever I send them to Norm.

I wrote out Reasons #1-3 and sat back, staring at them on the yellow notepad on my desk. I don't know. They didn't sound too convincing, to tell you the truth. I mean, the picture they were painting (speaking of painting) was of a selfish dude who just wanted to get his Ding-a-Ling off. That's true, I'm not denying it, but then I realized it's not *what* (getting off) that counts but *how* you get off (the right way or by running away?). That got me thinking again about Meant-to-Be and omens and Norm and penguins and *per aspera ad astra* and getting shot through the heart, and I did the only thing that a guy like me could do at a time like this. I screamed, out loud.

I really did. I sat there at my desk with the window open overlooking the gravel driveway on the side of the house and let out a good one. I didn't know what else to do. Afterward, it was quiet, the kind of quiet you can tell people are waiting to see if anything else is coming. I pictured mom and Kornél at the kitchen table playing gin rummy and suddenly freezing. That's when I thought of something even more terrible. What if all the running I've been doing is just running *away* from things instead of facing them the right way? But if that's true, then what is the right way? I'm asking, seriously. Here I do all this talking about morality and I don't even know right from wrong, but isn't that what morality is supposed to do, supposed to teach you?

I would have ended the entry for today at that last line above except for Amazing Thing #5 happening, which could be the GRANDDADDY of all the Amazing Things. Mom must have gotten really worried about my screaming and all, because she came into my room (that almost never happens) and said to me, "Richard, do you want to invite your friend to dinner with us on Tuesday? Your father wants to go to Ming's for the buffet."

"What?"

"The buffet."

"Why?"

"You know how he likes the fried dumplings."

"No, I mean who."

"Your father."

"Mom, who do you want me to invite?"

"Your friend," she said.

"Tommy?"

"No, the girl, Leslie."

I sat there staring at her. It was like this thing had taken on a life of its own. I couldn't even talk.

"Don't worry. Your father told me all about her. He's very happy that you two had that talk, you know, about things."

I cleared my throat.

"Her name's Laura."

"Laura, okay, so invite her to dinner on Tuesday. We'll have a nice time all of us together."

"But I don't know if she'll come."

"Invite her. She'll come."

"How do you know?"

"You're a handsome boy, Richard. Don't worry about the girls."

She turned to leave but I couldn't let her go without asking. "Mom, did dad tell you anything else?"

She thought for a minute and said, "You mean like that Indian show you're taking her to?"

"Indian show?"

"With the arrows."

"Yeah, that's the one."

"No, he didn't say a word."

Then she left, going back down the rickety steps to the kitchen. For the longest time I sat there staring at the doorway. I couldn't believe this was happening. There was no turning back now, even if I wanted to. So much for Fact Four: keeping my home life and Fedora life as far apart as possible. Was that ever really going to happen?

Tuesday, August 3
Ming's

Ming's is this old Chinese restaurant on Spring Garden not far from the house, and even though it's kind of dumpy, it's way better than 7615 Kingsbury, so I'm not complaining. I would have died if dinner had been at our house. Ming's is owned by this Chinese guy, Benny Ming, who wears the same blue jacket with a black tee-shirt underneath no matter the season or temperature outside. He slicks his hair back and always makes this joke about how it's a DA ("Duck's Ass") and that they're going to add it to the menu ("Peking DA"). Then he laughs hysterical and says, "Nah, not adding, just joking...Same booth?" But the place is pretty cool. It's red all over and has chandeliers with red and gold streamers and fish tanks with lobsters that have their claws taped together and scenes of rice paddies and acrobats on the walls. The booths are the color of green tea and in the summer the air is always blasting, which I like. There's this one waitress we always get, Alice Mong, whose Chinese name is Ming like the restaurant, but when I asked her once if Ming Mong was anything like King Kong, she just stared at me and said, "spring roll or wonton?" The spring rolls at Ming's are great. I always get the Spring Garden Spring Roll, which in the summer they call the Spring Garden Summer Roll and make twice as big. I dip it in a combo of sweet sauce and hot mustard. That's that sweet and sour thing I was telling you about. It's terrific, but you've got to get the balance just right, which takes practice. Too much sweet sauce and it's like eating lumpy syrup. Too much mustard and the top of your head will blow off. That happened to me a couple of times. It's not nice, believe me. Felt like somebody ripped my scalp off my skull.

Anyway, when I called Laura and invited her, she was excited and said how she'd been wanting to meet my family for the longest time and especially Kornél after talking to him on the phone. Then she was practically jumping up and down when I told her about the concert tickets. She said that Enz was going, too, and that we could ride with him and Ronnie Taglia (Purple Head) in the Corvair. Then she asked if Enz could come to dinner, since he would be driving her anyway (nobody touches his steering wheel except him), and wouldn't it be great all of us together. I said sure thing, great. I didn't say, maybe you could show us how you shave him. Is Ronnie coming, too? We got there first, which gave me a chance to survey the land. While mom was warning Benny about the hazards of air conditioning and asking how often did he change the filters (you're supposed to change them? he asked), Laura and Enz showed up. I could see them standing by the hostess station, Laura peering around the lobsters to see if she could see us. I slid down into the booth and pretended not to notice, but Kornél saw them right away and waved his arms like he was stranded on an island and had just seen a plane.

"Mom, dad, this is Laura and her brother, Enzo," I said when they came over. I stood up but was so nervous I dragged a corner of the tablecloth with me and spilled some water.

"Here, let me help you with that," Enz said, grinning.

They shook hands and then I introduced Kornél, who stood up and said in this big voice, "Welcome to Ming's, Home of the World Famous Benny's Barbequed Beef!" (It says it on a banner out front). Everybody laughed, including Benny, and then Laura and Enz joined us. Laura slid into the booth first, I followed, and Enz was last. After Benny left and Alice took our drink order, there was this long pause and then dad said to Laura, "So, Richard tells me you're a reporter on the school paper."

"That's right, Mister Mercurius. We're going to work on a story together about the old Philadelphia Athletics."

"Is that right?"

"Yes. We even watched them tearing down Connie Mack Stadium a few weeks ago."

"That must have been something. There's nothing like a wrecking ball to get the old blood pumping. All that demolition and crunching—fantastic!"

"But then it started to rain so we had to leave."

"Oh, you don't like getting wet?" I asked.

"We had nonno with us," she said, ignoring me. "That's my grandfather. We didn't want him to catch cold. He hasn't been feeling well lately."

"That's very nice of you," mom said. "See, she's a nice girl, looking after the nonno and her brother."

"Thank you," Laura said.

"She's a sweetheart," I said.

"Richard, don't be smart."

There it was, the first slap-down of the evening. I had been slapped down in the space of two minutes. Must have been a record.

Okay, fine. I probably shouldn't have been a smartass, cause I could tell Laura had gone out of her way to make a good impression. She had a pretty dress on, kind of like the sundress from church only dark blue with white smudges all over it like polka-dots and a red leather belt. She wore makeup, too, not a lot but just enough to look sophisticated and even sexy, which I bet dad could appreciate. She had different sandals on, plain sole with a braided leather strap, also red. I could smell them from where I sat. *This little piggy went to market, this little piggy stayed home.*

"So, Enzo, what do you do? Are you in school?" dad asked.

"No, I graduated three years ago. I work for our father at our car dealership. We own Fedora Auto Sales and Transport on South Street. I'm a mechanic there." Enz took out a Monopoly Man business card and handed it to dad, who looked at it, turned it over, and held it up to the light of the chandelier.

"Sixteen point, dull cover, matte finish."

"You know about paper?"

"A little. I used to work with my brother-in-law at a printer's here in Philadelphia. I helped him on the press."

"But you don't do it anymore?"

"No, that was a while ago. I've moved onto other things since then. But I'm glad to hear you're a mechanic, cause we've been having car trouble lately."

"Oh, really? What kind of car do you have?"

"A Chevy Estate Wagon, but it's got some mileage on it."

"What year?"

"Sixty-nine."

"Well, it's definitely time to trade up," Enz said. "We could cut you a deal, give you a good price on a trade-in."

"Oh, no," mom said. "I love that car. It has all the room in the world and I feel safe in it. It'll run till the cows come home."

"Well, if you change your mind, you know where we are. And you can bring it in anytime for service. I'll work on it myself."

"That's nice. Isn't that nice?" mom said. "He's a nice young man."

Somehow, she had decided that "nice" was the word of the day. It was like she got a dollar every time she used it. Then Kornél, holding up a small jar of sweet and sour sauce, announced to everyone in the restaurant, "Look, Laura's hair is the color of Chinese gravy!" He calls everything gravy, even syrup. The only thing he doesn't call gravy is gravy.

"*Kornél!*"

"No, that's all right. I don't mind," Laura said. "It's kinda cute. Yes, I guess my hair is the color of gravy."

"Your hair is beautiful," mom said. "So where is it from, your mother or father?"

"My father. He has the same red hair."

"Enzo, you must take after your mother, then."

"I guess, except she's got a pretty hot temper. Her family's Sicilian."

"Richard takes after his father, but neither one will admit it. They're not hot-tempered but very stubborn. Smart but stubborn. That's Hungarian."

"Thanks, mom."

"You're welcome, dah-ling."

"Dah-ling" was not a word I heard often and was reserved for special occasions, usually to impress people, distinguish our family from the rest of America, or just because mom was in the mood to sound like Zsa Zsa Gábor. That last one didn't make a whole lot of sense, because mom was anything but glamorous. I mean, I love her and all that, but I don't picture her in magazines or on TV. Besides, I can't see any of those Gábor sisters working for Bell of Pennsylvania. They'd chip their nails.

Alice brought over the drinks (the Real Thing for Enz, Uncola for Laura—just to be different—iced-tea for me), and then dad said, "Okay, everybody ready? Let's hit the buffet," which made us sound like Marines storming the beach. After we filed through the line and got back to the booth, I decided to try something bold, go for it, you know, just like the Marines. After all, that's what *per aspera ad astra* is all about. I waited till Laura was well into her Chicken Ming with Cashews, and then I slid my left hand down beside me on the booth and kept it there. It was easy, since I'm right-handed and have gotten pretty good eating with chopsticks. I think chopsticks must have been invented by some guy who wanted to free up one hand for other things, maybe just like this. Besides, I got Roast Beef Egg Foo Young, which is pretty easy to handle. *This little piggy had roast beef.*

"So, how do you like Saint Rita's?" dad asked Laura after polishing off the fried dumplings and digging into that world famous barbeque.

"Oh, it's great. I really like the school."

"What about studying with boys? You don't mind that? You know, there was quite a big to-do about it going coed."

"No, I actually like it. The boys are all right. They leave us alone. Besides, the teachers are all very helpful. It's like they go out of their way to make sure you understand the material."

"That's good to hear. Richard's had the same experience, especially with that French teacher. What's her name? I met her last year at the open house."

"Missus Dudoit," I answered.

"The French teacher."

"Missus Dudoit."

"What?"

"Du—doit, like droit du roi."

"That's it. Anyway, she wore a long, flowing scarf and had rings on every finger. I thought she was a Gypsy."

"Oh, Robi, don't exaggerate," mom said, looking around the table.

"Who's exaggerating? The woman jiggled and jangled every time she moved."

"That doesn't mean she's a Gypsy. Besides, you only met her once."

"Once was enough. I need more time?"

"No, you just need to know not everybody who looks Gypsy is Gypsy, especially nowadays. There're Gypsies all over the place."

"But that's my point."

"What?"

"How was I supposed to know?"

"Know what?"

"That she wasn't a Gypsy?"

It went on like this with mom defending the "Romenies" and dad saying how he wasn't trying to insult them or anything, and then something about how they get together every May in Southern France for some big reunion and he just thought that Mrs. Dudoit was one of them, what with her teaching French and having a Frenchy last name and don't make such a big deal out of it, etc., etc.. How was he supposed to know? I took advantage of the distraction and made my move. I put my hand on Laura's thigh and squeezed a little, not too much, just enough for her to know what I had in mind. I figured it was safe since it was under the table and Enz was on my other side. I was pretty sure he couldn't see anything.

And then something happened. I can't say it was amazing and should be added to the list of Amazing Things, but I can't say I didn't like it, either, even though it made me look bad. Above all, it was funny, and I have to give credit where credit is due. Sure, I'm the Merk and I'm a funny guy, but I can appreciate it when somebody gets my goat, which is what Laura did. Got me good. With my hand resting on her thigh, she calmly took a spoon, scooped up some of that special Chicken Ming gravy, and poured it out on my hand. I don't know how she did it without anybody seeing, but it was warm and lumpy. What she didn't count on was my reaction, which was to be just as calm and do nothing. I didn't even flinch, and when the gravy started oozing from my hand onto her dress, she put her hand on top of mine to stop it. That's when I grabbed her fingers so tight that we were having a tug-of-war under the table. She tried to wiggle away, but our fingers became entwined in a slimy love knot of Chicken Ming gravy. It was the sexiest thing I've ever done with mom and dad in the room.

"So, Laura, why don't you tell us how you and Richard met?" mom said with a look like she knew exactly what was going on.

"All right," Laura said. "Well, there was a meeting of the newspaper staff in Mister Andrade's office at the end of school—he's our advisor—and we were sitting there talking about how the sports editor was moving to Arizona and that that was a real problem, because we didn't know who could cover the football team's training camp in August. The only person who knew the team and the players was the same guy who was writing the lead story about Vice Principal Novak."

"Who was that?"

I squeezed her hand.

"Richard. But then he was late to the meeting, so we decided that the only thing we could do to save the paper was to have Richard cover the training camp and we would do the vice principal story in the winter."

"That's when you met?"

"No. He still wasn't at the meeting, so I said well, if it means scrapping the lead story, I'd volunteer to write it so we could keep everything as planned and not have to rework the layout. Glenn, the editor agreed, and so did the other reporters."

"And that's when you met?"

"Yes. Richard finally showed up all out of breath and sweating and got really upset that we made the decision without him. He wanted his assignment back. But it was too late for that, so he was mad at me for the rest of the meeting."

"See, stubborn."

"But that was on a Friday and Richard came to see me that Sunday to apologize. It was very nice of him."

There was that word again, "nice," although this time it wasn't half bad. In fact, Laura squeezed *my* hand. I finally came out smelling like a rose, even if it was a total lie. I could see mom liked it, too. Nice is nice.

"Ever been to the shrine?" dad said suddenly.

We stopped and looked over at him. He was just coming down from the ceiling with a question for us about something or other that no one had a clue about. *Please, God, don't let him go whacko, please!*

"Shrine, Robi?" mom asked.

"The Saint Rita of Cascia Shrine. It's three blocks from the high school on South Broad."

"Oh, that shrine. No."

"We have," Enz said.

"What? No we haven't," Laura said.

"Sure, we have. Mom took us there every Sunday afternoon. You were just a kid, so I guess you don't remember."

"Really? Why?"

Enz shrugged. "How should I know?"

"Do you know the story of Saint Rita?" dad asked. "It's very interesting."

"A little bit," Enz said. "There's something about a rose, a thorn, and a feud. Mom used to say she had a special devotion to Saint Rita and that if she ever had another girl, she'd name her Rita, which is short for Margherita."

"That's right. You may not know it, but there aren't a whole lot of married saints in the church, and Saint Rita is one of them. But her marriage was awful. Her husband was an abusive man with a violent temper who belonged to one of the two most powerful families in Cascia in Italy. They were constantly at war with each other. Eventually, he was stabbed to death and Rita's two sons died of dysentery. Rita, who had lived with her husband's abuse and infidelities for years, entered an Augustinian convent and lived there until she died. She's the patron saint of abused women, impossible causes, and reconciliation, even though the reconciliation with her husband was short-lived."

"Well, I guess now you know why mom went there," Enz said, leaning past me to look at Laura.

"That's a stupid thing to say!"

"Why? It's true."

"Is not."

"Is so."

"Is not!"

Laura made a face and pulled her hand away from mine, wiping it with a napkin. Then, just as I was about to say how much I enjoyed going over to the Fedoras, what a great family they were, and how the spirit of St. Rita was alive and well through the obvious feelings of *Veritas, Unitas,* and *Caritas!* (blah, blah, blah, blah, blah), Kornél yelled, "Dad, finish the story!"

"That's everything."

"What about the rose and thorn?"

"Right, those are also very interesting. See, every saint has to have some kind of proof that they're a saint, and Saint Rita has the rose and thorn. They say that when she was dying she asked for a rose from her garden, but since it was in the middle of winter, they told her there weren't any. But she insisted, and when they went to look, sure enough there was a rose in full bloom. So they gave it to her."

"And the thorn?"

"One day when she was praying in front of a crucifix, a thorn from Christ's crown came down and struck her in the forehead and left a mark on her till the day she died. They call it a mark or stigma of Christ's crucifixion."

"Mark?"

"That's right. They also call it her 'Wound of Love.'"

Kornél thought for a moment, looked down at his plate and then up at the ceiling. He was either imitating dad, making fun of him, or it was genetic, which wasn't so good for me.

"Like Damien?" he said.

"Who's Damien?"

"From *The Omen.*"

"The movie?"

"Yeah, he had a mark. I want to see it!"

"No, it's too scary. You'll have nightmares."

"*Please, please?* Richard can take me and Laura can come, too. She'll love it. Right, Laura, you'll love it?"

"You know, I haven't seen it yet and I'd love to go, but I've been waiting for Richard to ask me," Laura said.

Before I could pass out under the table, mom said, "Good thing you said it now, Laura, otherwise you'll be waiting forever. Richard's a good boy, but he's a Mercurius and the Mercurius men don't understand anything, believe me."

"Me, too?" Kornél asked.

"I'm sorry, dah-ling."

Slap-down number two, a serious one this time, from my own mother. With a mother like this, who needs Rose Fedora? And yet, she was just saying out loud what I've been writing about all along.

"So, dad, since we don't get anything, maybe we could change all of that by you giving me something," I said.

"Like what?"

"The car to drive Laura to the movies."

"And Kornél!" Kornél yelled.

"If dad lets you," I said.

"Laura, do you have a license?"

"Yes, Mister Mercurius."

"Ever been in an accident?"

"No, sir."

"Do you take drugs?"

"Absolutely not."

"All right, then, as long as you're careful and I don't have to have the car towed to Enzo's shop."

"Thanks, dad."

"You're welcome, Richard. So, that's what the gas money was for. I should have known."

"What about me?" Kornél said.

"Sure, go ahead, but if you get scared and wet the bed, Richard has to help you change the sheets. Now, who's ready for round two?"

This was incredible. I now had a second date with Laura even before the first one, which was great news because we were already in August and I had a deadline to meet (I don't mean football camp).[14] So we were definitely on-again, maybe even permanently this time. Of course, the girl liked horror movies. What else would a Fedora like, especially now that Big Al's exploits were out in the open and we saw how the Feds (my new name for them) really operate? Guess he had his own version of a Summer roll! I was so excited that when everybody got up for seconds, I dropped my napkin on purpose so I could crawl underneath the table to smell Laura's feet. The leather had a straw smell and her toenails were freshly painted red. I closed my eyes, inhaled, and almost passed out. This was too good to be true. Then, at the end of the meal when Alice brought the orange slices and fortune cookies over, mine said, "A journey of a thousand miles begins with a single step." Oh, yeah it does, an instep.

---

14 Question: How do you count the order here? Is the concert date first, because it was planned first and I already bought the tickets even though it hasn't happened yet? Or is the movie date first, because it will come before the concert even though we just thought of it at dinner tonight and I haven't bought the tickets yet? How do you decide stuff like this? Footnote to the footnote: I'm beginning to see just how important order is. For instance, what would have happened if Kornél had been born first and me second? He'd be me and I'd be him and there would be no Laura Fedora, at least not in our lives. There might not even be a Ming's.

Thursday, August 5
No Atticus Finch

We ended up going to the 7:15 pm show at The Pearl, which isn't far from our house on Kingsbury. I tried to pick a theatre closer to Laura's, but when you have to borrow a car and have half a license, you're kind of at the mercy of people who don't share your same sense of urgency to get laid. That's what we're talking about, right? That's what all this is for, so why pretend? I want to do it, Laura is waiting for me to do it, the four adults are trying to stop me, and Kornél just wants to see a movie.

Anyway, Laura took the bus to our house, I drove us to The Pearl, dad didn't have to tow the car to Big Al's, and Kornél got to see *The Omen*, which was a stupid movie about a rotten little kid who's just like every other kid and not the antichrist, unless, of course, they all are, which I am not ruling out after working at the Day Camp for six weeks. And Gregory Peck was no Atticus Finch, either, what with getting ripped up by evil dogs. But my point is that everybody got what they wanted except me. Am I being a brat like Damien pedaling around the house on his squeaky tricycle? Maybe, but what about the ultimate humiliation of going on a date with your kid brother? Might as well have had nonno with us to hock loogies all through the movie. And the surprise ending that everybody's been talking about was no surprise at all, otherwise how are they going to make *Omen* II, III, and IV? But the worst part was that there was no sex in the movie, not even a flashed boob or thigh. What am I supposed to do with that? I guess it doesn't matter, cause even though Laura sat next to me with Kornél on her other side, she spent most of the movie taking care of him, making sure he had enough soda and Raisinets. Then, of course, he spilled the Raisinets, which meant we had to go on a scavenger hunt in the dark to save the good ones. So I guess not having sex in the movie was no big deal. I was hoping that watching people do it on screen would have been a great turn-on for the two of us, but whatever turn-on there might have been was cancelled out by Kornél being there. So there he was ruining my life again, except this time I didn't feel guilty over the whole louse thing.

There was one good thing that happened, though, and it got me so fired up I came right back after seeing Laura home to write this entry. It occurred to me in a *coup de foudre* (corrected from *coup d'état*) that the priest in the movie (not the one with the eyeball but the other one with the crucifix who gets speared by the lightning rod) looked a lot like Mr. Andrade, which I took as a sign (omen!) from God that I should ask Mr. Andrade to borrow his car for my Great Escape. How perfect is that? I happen to know he has two cars, one his regular one that he drives to work and parks out front of the school, and another he hardly uses and leaves covered up in the faculty parking lot. I've seen him go out in winter every Friday afternoon to turn the engine over and rev it. He'd probably let me borrow it. Why not? I know my Shakespeare. Then I could do this thing with a clear conscience, since I don't want to screw anybody over by stealing something they really need like money or medicine or credit cards. You know, stuff like that. That would be a sin, but taking something extra doesn't hurt anybody and will help me get to my goal. It may not be the most moral of things, but drastic times require drastic measures. Besides, I think Norm would approve. If I make it big firefighting, I'll repay Mr. Andrade by sending him monthly installments. How much could an old car cost, anyway? Maybe I should check with Enz just to be sure.

It was interesting seeing Laura home on the bus. She really appreciated my doing it and was very thankful (not thankful enough, but thankful). It was interesting, but I am not going to make a separate category for Interesting Things, because this journal is already getting filled up with notes and drawings that get in the way of the main story. And I can't let that happen, not in this journal and not in life. You've got to stick to the main story, or you'll end up lost. I know that much. It's like keeping your eye on the ball. So the interesting thing that happened is that walking to her house from the bus stop, we held hands and it was great, especially in the dark. Her hands were soft and our fingers fit together perfect, nice this time and not like under the table at Ming's. There was even a breeze that rustled the leaves of the sycamore trees in the park. But then, just outside her house when I leaned forward to kiss her, she stepped back.

"What?"

"Not now, I can't."

"Yes you can. Your family's inside. They can't see us, and there's nobody else around. I checked."

"It's not that."

"What, then?"

She hesitated.

"You don't want to?" I asked.

"No, I do."

"Really?"

"Yeah."

So, I leaned forward again, close to her face, ready to plant the BIG ONE.

"No," she said, pushing me back.

"Why not?"

"It's not time. It has to be special."

I looked at her, not sure if she was pulling my leg, but it was too dark to tell.

"Special? So, when will it be special?"

"We'll just know. You can't plan these things. You have to let them happen on their own. When it's time, we'll know. By the way, come over Saturday afternoon and we'll go up to Valley Forge with Enz and Deborah. They're planning a picnic. Bye, gotta go!"

She turned and went inside, the aluminum door with the "F" swooshing closed. I stood there thinking this is one confusing girl.

Saturday, August 7
The BIG ONE

I did my chores, which were hosing out the garbage cans, mowing the backyard (Kornél helped me rake the clippings), pulling weeds in the garden, and, since Kornél is about as blind as a bat when it comes to throwing rocks at squirrels, replacing the smashed window in the garage door. Believe it or not, I finished by noon. The guy at the hardware store had the right size window, and it was even on sale—two for one—which mom liked. When I finished, I showered, put on some of dad's English Leather (it stung), and wore my favorite bellbottoms with a clean red-and-white striped t-shirt. Pretty sharp, I thought, till mom said, "What, you joining the Navy all of a sudden?" Good one. As Rose Fedora says, "I'm living in a house of comedians." But it got me wondering whether I should have worn the blue shorts with my school polo shirt instead. What do you wear to a picnic? I should follow Enz's example, I guess. He knows how to dress. But I did pack the two condoms I've been saving from Hilene Katzenbaum's End-of-School-Pool-Party. I got them from her brother Jerry, who also came up with the idea for the theme: "From Pool to Pool" (the Katzenbaum's have a pool table in their rec room). That wasn't bad, but not nearly as smart as what I thought up: "From Rack to Rack." Get it?

When I got to Laura's, she opened the door and let me in. She was wearing white short shorts that somehow got stuck in my throat and a yellow blouse tied in the front that left her stomach uncovered. I was glad they had air conditioning, because without it I would have fainted. We went into the kitchen where Mrs. Fedora stood over a frying pan burning scrapple, her hair in curlers and a cigarette hanging out of her mouth. The fan above the stove was on high. Before she could ask if we wanted any, Laura led me downstairs to nonno's room, where they had been listening to records. The room had cement walls and cellar windows filled with plants and old wine bottles, the jug kind. Magazines, books, and records of all kinds were stacked like stalagmites all around. There was even one of those old phonographs, the kind with the dog and hand crank, in a corner of the room. Nonno stood next to a stack of books, his eyes closed, waving his hands to the music.

"He's conducting," Laura said.

"With his hat on?"

"It's his favorite. Frank Sinatra gave it to him after a concert when he told him his name was Fedora. Besides, he doesn't like the cold and he hates air conditioning."

"He'd get along with my mother, then."

"Why, does she like Sinatra?"

"Well, yeah but—"

Without waiting for me to finish, she sat down on the bed, which was lumpy and covered with a handmade quilt. On the wall above the headboard were rosary beads as big as Christmas balls. Photos of Italian tenors were all around the room, some with names, others without. "Franco Corelli," "Enrico Caruso," "Beniamino Gigli." I recognized Mario Lanza from the movies. Laura picked up an album cover and started reading it. Her hair was loose, her legs tanned and shaved, and she wore plain leather sandals. She had been sweating in them, I could tell.

"You look nice," I said.

"Thank you." Then, *"Merk, what are you wearing?"*

"What?"

"Is that perfume?"

"No, cologne, English Leather. Do you like it?"

She grunted something and leaned into me to take a whiff. "It's okay." Then she went back to reading.

"So, when are we leaving?" I asked.

"As soon as Enz gets back. He went to pick up Deborah."

"Do we need anything? For the picnic, I mean."

"Nope, got it covered."

"Cole slaw?"

"Yep."

"Hot dogs and hamburgers?"

"Chicken."

"How about drinks?"

"Enz's buying beer and wine right now. I also made Ambrosia."

"What's that?"

"Fruit salad mixed with marshmallows and coconut. I think you'll like it."

"Sounds great."

"I want to make sure you have sweet lips," she said without looking up.

"Does that mean it's time?"

"Maybe, you never know. I don't plan things, but I want to be prepared. Speaking of sweet lips, here, try this!"

She poured some clear liquid into a small glass and handed it to me. There was no way I was falling for that again.

"No, thanks. I already tried that stuff. It's awful!"

"It's not grappa, silly, it's Sambuca."

"Who?"

"Just try it."

She stood in front of me till I took it and swallowed. It was thick and sweet like licorice, but it burned going down. Then she took it back and swallowed the rest, laughing. Nonno laughed, too. This was starting to feel like my dream. I looked around for a typewriter and revolver. I wondered if maybe the Feds were the way they were because they combined things in unnatural ways, like scrapple and Sambuca. And even though there was a certain logic to it—both starting with "S"—it was too unnatural to be right. It was like a two-headed turtle, possible, sure, but not the way things were meant to be.

"Uh-oh, he's doing it again," Laura said.

"Doing what?"

Nonno went over to the stereo, took the record off that had been playing, and put on a new one. I didn't notice anything at first and used the time to hold Laura's hand, this time kissing her fingers, which she let me do.[15] But after a while the music changed, and even though I couldn't tell where it was from, I swore I'd heard it before.

"It's 'Hello Muddah, Hello Fadduh,'" Laura said. "You know, that song about the kid at camp who wants to go home."

"Oh, right."

"The music is 'Dance of the Hours' by Amilcare Ponchielli. Nonno plays it all the time. I mean *all* the time."

She showed me the album cover. As far as I knew, Amilcare Ponchielli was something you used for diaper rash, but I didn't say so. Then nonno turned the volume up and started dancing in place, which was more like shuffling. It didn't take long for Rose to come to the top of the stairs and yell, "Turn that crap down, old man!" He yelled something back, rasping, and turned the volume up more.

"I'll kill you, Henny! God help me, I'll kill you!"

When the music got to the chase scene, he turned it up as high as it could go, left it there for half a minute, and then lowered it to where it was practically nothing. There was silence from upstairs, and I thought about last week when I screamed and you could have heard a pin drop. Then he sat down on the bed, exhausted.

"His name is Henny?"

"Enrico, but my mother calls him Henny."

I looked at her.

"It's just a thing they do," she said.

Enz showed up not much later with Deborah, who wore a floppy hat with a denim skirt and another blouse that tied in the front and showed off her butternut squash harvest, which was fine with me. I made sure neither Enz nor Laura caught me staring. It

---

15 *I get it now. It's lips that make a kiss, not any other body part. And it has to be four lips, not two. Kiss = 4 lips touching, with or without tongue. Peck = lips to cheek. Anything else is just European.*

was all right if Deborah did, though, because I like to flirt. There's no harm in that, is there? It seemed like Mrs. Fedora and Deborah had met before, because they were very chatty. Chatty Cathies. We loaded up the Corvair, and—guess what?—it didn't break down. We said our goodbyes and cruised along Vine Street and the Schuylkill Expressway with the top down, past the Art Museum, toward Conshohocken. I was in the back with Laura, who let me put my arm around her as she snuggled up next to me, her hair smelling every bit like it did at the stadium, except this time it blew straight into my face. Up front, Deborah was all over Enz like ivy around a tree, and I had the feeling that they had already done it and were headed up to Valley Forge to do more of it, which was also all right by me. I figure that's what summer's for (that's what Big Al said!). So, with the radio on, we flew down the Schuylkill, passing cars on either side and having a great time. I felt so much like an adult that it wasn't funny—free without a worry in the world and even thinking how great it would be just Laura and me escaping from everything and everybody. So no way did I feel bad about taking her away from her family or me running away from mine even if it felt wrong every once in a while, because right now it was the right thing to do.

I have to tell you, Valley Forge on a Saturday afternoon in August is something to see. I had no idea there would be so many tourists. There were crowds all over the place, from the Welcome Center where there was a lecture by a "renowned Goschenhoppen historian" with stringy brown hair to the huge Memorial Arch, which had a Shoofly Pie Bake-Off and Eating Contest (no lie), to the Von Steuben Statue on the other side of the park. There were families with strollers and broad-brimmed hats, kids running around with balloons and flags, packs of cyclists, busloads of well-dressed Japanese tourists with umbrellas and cameras, near naked joggers, history nerds, guys with powder and muskets, women dressed like Hester Prynne, blacksmiths, cobblers, walking tours, and a fife and drum corps with an enormous fat guy playing the fife. He was so big it looked like a harmonica. We argued for a while about where to go, but Deborah had already planned it all out, so we drove to the far side of Washington's Headquarters, where it was a little quieter and there was a hillside overlooking a creek that ran down to the Schuylkill River. Enz parked in the shade and we started unloading.

"Tell you what," he said. "You girls take the blankets and find a spot, we'll follow you with the rest of the stuff."

As soon as they left, he took off his fancy Ray Bans and said to me with a really serious face, "Okay, Merk, here's the deal. We'll sit down together, eat, have some fun, and then me and Deborah are gonna disappear. You and Laura stay with the food and stuff close to the car. You got that?" He looked at me like this was a matter of life and death.

"Sure."

"And you better treat her right."

"Who, Laura?"

"No, Betsy fucking Ross."

"Oh, right. Of course I will."

He looked at me even more serious. "Good."

We carried the baskets of chicken, beans, Cole slaw, corn, and Ambrosia salad along with two six-packs of Genny Cream Ale and a cold bottle of sangria plus all the silverware and napkins (were they feeding the troops?) to the spot the girls had picked out in the shade of a sassafras tree. I knew it was a sassafras tree, cause there was a label stuck in the dirt at the base that said, "Laura-ceae/Sassafras/Sassafras albidum," which I figured was God's way of telling me, "Right on, Merk!" There it was in Black & White— the tree was called "Laura." There were also some snowball bushes around, white and purple. That's what we call them, but I don't know their real name. The sassafras was the real thing, though.

"See that, Laura? They named a tree after you."

"Cool," she said, unpacking the baskets.

"Merk, pass me a beer, would you," Enz said.

I popped one open and handed it to him. He rolled the bottle across his forehead, took a long swig, and then stretched out against Deborah, staring up at the clouds. Somehow, he didn't strike me as the dreamer type, but there he was apparently thinking.

"Enz, mind if I have one?"

"That's what they're there for."

I helped myself and offered one to Deborah, then Laura, but Laura was busy making plates for everybody. "You need help?" I asked.

"Nope. I got it. I'm giving you extra Ambrosia."

"That's great."

"Laura made it, you know," I said, turning toward Deborah, who smiled. "So, you're in med school?"

"No, pre-med. I'm a bio student," she said.

"Where?"

"Temple. It's near the café where I work."

"So, what are you studying?"

I didn't mean it the way it came out. I was thinking of different kinds of medicine like intestines, heart, breasts, surgery, crazy people, kids, Ears-Nose-Throat (I always thought it was strange how they bunched those together but nothing else. Why not Feet-Toes-Ankles, Head-Neck-Eyes, Legs-Thighs-Privates, *Head-Shoulders-Knees-and-Toes*)? But it was too late to take back. Enz sat up and looked at me, Laura stopped plopping Cole slaw onto a paper plate, and Deborah just stared back.

"Biology," she said.

"Oh, right."

"What, you forgot?" Enz said, snickering.

"Leave him alone, Enz, he's just making conversation," Laura said.

"That's right, pick on somebody your own size," Deborah said.

"Are you my size?" Enz asked her.

"No, but you're mine."

"Oh yeah?"

This got the two of them giggling, which got them horsing around, which got them kissing, which got them whispering to each other about who knows what. Then Deborah pried herself loose and adjusted her bosoms. By then Laura had made all the plates (she pretended not to see or hear anything), and we sat there for a while eating and drinking beer: Enz and Deborah on one blanket, Laura and me on another close to the sassafras tree. Where else? We were going to make our own sassy-frassy, I thought. But then Laura looked mad, which made me think she was jealous of Deborah and that Laura and her brother really were doing more than shaving with all that cream. On the other hand, maybe she just had more scruples than Enz, who seemed to be driven by one thing and one thing only (the dog!). Then scruple reminded me of scrapple, which reminded me of Sambuca and sangria. If to that you added sassafras, you'd get Scruple-Scrapple-Sambuca-Sangria-Sassafras, which was better than winning the lottery. That's how I think, like way out sometimes. I guess I am related to my old man. I am also variable.

"Penny for your thoughts?" Laura said.

"What?"

"You've been quiet. What are you thinking about?"

"I dunno, stuff."

"Stuff?"

"Yeah."

"You know, you should join the debate team," she said.

"Yeah, I get that a lot. They asked me, but I turned them down."

"Very funny."

Finally, it was time for *our* horseplay, which I did by doing the Itsy-Bitsy-Spider routine I pulled the other day on Kornél, moving my fingers slowly up her arm to her shoulder. She let me get that far but then shoved my hand away. I looked over at Enz, who had all of a sudden looked up, so I backed down.

"Listen, we're going for a little walk," he said, standing up.

"Where to?" asked Laura.

"On the Horse-Shoe Trail. It's right over there."

"But we were going to play Frisbee."

"You two play. Have fun!"

He winked at me, then took the bottle of sangria and walked hand-in-hand with Deborah up the slope that led to the head of the trail. When they were out of sight, Laura said, "My brother's a pothead. He thinks I don't know, but I'm not stupid." There was a pause and then she said, "Merk, you ever feel like running away?" Holy crap! I didn't say anything, *couldn't* say anything. It's like she had read my mind. *Did she read my journal, too?*

"I mean, just getting away from it all and not looking back?" she said.

"Are you kidding? All the time."

"Then let's do it! Let's run away you and me and live together for the rest of our lives!"

I stuttered for the third time in my life.

"Are you serious?"

"Why not?"

"I thought you wanted to stay here."

"I never said that."

"You didn't?"

"No, maybe you dreamt it," she said.

This was getting weird. "But we haven't kissed yet."

"So kiss me."

"It's time?"

"You know what Elvis says."

"I'm itchin like a man up a fuzzy tree?"

"No, it's now or never."

"Okay."

I moved slowly into position. I wasn't sure if it was better to sit or kneel, so I scrunched up close to her and leaned in.

"No, not here," she said.

Here we go again. "Then where?"

"Where it's private," she said, nodding toward the sassafras tree. What was it with this girl and trees? She'll have no trouble in a tree house, that's for sure.

We went to the tree and she sat down with her back against the trunk. I didn't want to give her a chance to change her mind, so I leaned forward right away and we did it—the BIG ONE, the smooch, the lip lock, the *baccio* (I bought a pocket Italian dictionary). Her lips felt cool and moist and still tasted like licorice from the Sambuca. We kept at it long and deep until our tongues played with each other. When we finally came up for air, I was barely conscious

"I love you, Laura."

It got real quiet and in that one moment, in that short time that we sat there looking into each other's eyes, I meant it. I *loved* her. I really did and was so happy I could have died right then and there. I swear to God I was ready. I'm not making this up. I could have keeled over with a heart attack.

"You do?" she asked.

"With all my heart."

"I love you, too, Merk."

My throat got dry.

"But I want our love to be never-ending. Promise me it'll never end."

"It'll never end."

"No, not like that. You have to mean it."

"I mean it."

"Cross your heart?"

I crossed my heart.

"And hope to die?"

I wasn't about to go through that again, so I took her by the shoulders to kiss her again, but she said, "No, just hold me."

"Sure." I could feel the skin of her shoulders and lower back as we hugged. It was as smooth as olive oil. I couldn't believe this was happening. It was also obvious that I was getting excited, if you know what I mean. I wasn't sure what to do.

"Your family's nice, Merk, aren't they?" she asked after a while.

"My family?"

"Yeah, they seem like nice people."

"Uh, sure."

"They don't fight or anything, do they?"

"Fight, no. They're just strange."

"But your parents, they're faithful to each other and don't mess around or do stupid things, right?"

"No, nothing like that," I said, trying not to imagine my parents at a wife swapping party, which was exactly what I thought of: them with the Dudoits. It was the way dad had said "jiggled and jangled."

"I don't like betrayal, Merk. It's the worst thing that could happen to a person."

She looked at me, her eyes deep green like grass. Betrayal was bad, sure, but I figured there were at least two or three worse things, like being boiled alive. Ever since I read *Shōgun*, I've been terrified of getting stuck in the shower with the hot water turned on (the samurai used to boil people in oil).

"You wouldn't do that, would you?"

"God no," I said.

"Other people, adults, do it all the time, and it's disgusting."

"I know."

"And if you did it to me, I'd be crushed."

"I swear to you, Laura, I'll never cheat on you or boil you in oil."

"What?"

"I mean cheat on you, never."

"Not even with Darlene DeAngelo? I know what they say about her."

"Cross my heart."

"Just don't cross *my* heart," she said, which I thought was pretty witty, *touché* and all, until she added, "Or I'll cut yours out."

Now that really turned me on. I tried to kiss her again, but she jumped up and yelled, "Time for Frisbee!"

"Now?"

"Now."

So there she was, Laura being Laura again, and there wasn't anything I could do about it but chase the Frisbee around the meadow like a dog. She was good at it, I'll give her that. She could fling the thing with an underarm, sidearm snap that wasn't anything like a girl. A couple times she even threw it from behind her back.

"Enz taught me," she said.

So for the next hour we played Frisbee, drank beer, and ate more. We even fed each other chicken, which I thought was the sexiest thing ever and as good as being married. I felt good about everything, not just because we were *K-i-s-s-i-n-g* under a tree, but because I had told the truth. I may not know what love is, but I know what betrayal is, even if it isn't exactly the worst thing in the world. I remembered the look on Mrs. Fedora's face when Summer showed up, and I know I could never do that to Laura. See, our love wasn't unnatural like the Feds or a two-headed turtle. It was totally different. It was Meant-to-Be.

Sunday, August 8
Mass, the Variable I'm Constantly Thinking Of

I got up early and went with mom and Kornél to the 9:00 Mass, first, because I've been so excited ever since the BIG ONE that I can't sleep or eat or do much of anything else, and, second, because now that this is really going to happen (Wyoming), I wanted to ask

God's blessing on it. It might seem strange asking God to bless a kidnapping, but, dude, how many more confirmations do I need? If there were any more, I'd have to wear a red robe and get a sponsor. By my count, there are at least twelve: the five Amazing Things; my talk with dad about *per aspera ad astra;* Norm being from Wyoming; the tree house we'll live in (Laura'll go ape); the fortune cookie; the sassafras tree; the BIG ONE; and her wanting to run away with me and live together. For it to be any more obvious, Jesus would have to show up at Day Camp and tell me, "Look, Merk, you haven't been too quick on the uptake, so I'm gonna lay it out for you: TAKE THE GIRL TO WYOMING...!"[16] It'd be in red, too, cause everything he says is in red.

And it's what Laura wants. It's what she begged me for and what I think about day and night, night and day, and every minute in between, which I guess would be dusk and dawn, which isn't a bad name for a novel about a guy so in love that the only time he gets to eat and sleep is at dusk and dawn. So, now I've got a sixth title for my novel, which I decided to start right there in church, except that the coffee break and bake sale downstairs were so noisy with kids running around and old ladies in summer hats gabbing that I had to go back upstairs to the church and sit in a pew to get some peace. I even thought about naming the two lovers in *Dusk and Dawn* "Dusk" and "Dawn," which would be a terrific play on words. I could imagine guys years from now thanking me because their parents named them "Dusk" from the movie they make from my novel. It'd be the coolest name ever.

I sat in the middle of the pews on the right, because most people fill up the back first, and the people who go straight to the front and have conversations with the statues are scary. Sometimes they stand there yelling out loud until the sacristan, a guy in a black

---

16 *I have to believe that these balance out my dream about getting shot through the heart and Norm's worries about Friday the 13th. When it comes to that, the guy with the red shoes is completely wrong.*

robe named Csaba Kroski (everybody calls him Crotchy), has to calm them down or tell them to leave. I sat there thinking, writing notes for *Dusk and Dawn*, and studying the statues of Jesus, Mary, and St. Stephen, who is this bearded guy with a crown in charge of horses, coffin makers, and headaches, which I guess is what happens when your crown is too tight. I stared at the red flickering candles, the big marble pillars all around the church, and the dark wooden confessionals that look like upended coffins, taking it all in the way I sat there taking in my own living room. I must have lost track of time, because before I knew it the 11:00 Mass had begun. But I couldn't get out. I was hemmed in by a family with about fourteen kids on one side and a fat guy with a handlebar mustache and suspenders on the other. I was stuck in my second Mass of the day! The only other time I got stuck in two Masses was when mom sang at a wedding and I had to wait for her to drive me home. It was either that or sit up in the choir loft.

Okay, so I can't hold it in anymore and have to tell you something that, if not exactly an Amazing Thing, must be a Crazy Thing. Maybe not even that, because it's really personal, so personal that I have to wonder if I should just shut up about it and not let anyone know or even admit it to myself, because somehow if I write it down I might spontaneously combust. I might combust anyway. Still, it happened, and as an observer of human nature I have an obligation to tell the truth no matter how perverted. I mean, that's what all this writing and journaling are about, right? I have to come clean or else I'm a fraud, which I am not. With any luck, by the time somebody reads this I'll be dead and won't have to worry about the humiliation. What about my kids, though? What'll it do to them? Don't I have a moral obligation to protect them? I don't know. How am I supposed to think about kids when I'm fifteen and the only driving I'm used to is a stick-shift, not an automatic, if you catch my drift?

All right, here it is plain and simple. Well, maybe not as plain as vanilla and not simple by a long shot, but here it is anyway—*I got so excited during Mass that I came in my pants*—I'll wait a while for that to sink in. In fact, I have to go to the bathroom. I'll be back.

BATHROOM BREAK

Okay, I'm back. I was gone longer than I thought, because mom called from downstairs reminding me to take the garbage out and make sure I don't cut myself on the broken glass and then telling me how proud she is that I went to two Masses in one day. I guess I'm racking up points to get out of Purgatory, which must be like Jail (is there a Get-Out-of-Purgatory card?). Seriously, she says stuff like that all the time. But in this case she may not be too far off, because I'm going to need all the help I can get. All right, so here's what happened. I guess there's really no way to explain it (I don't know myself), so I'll just tell you the A-B-C of it and leave it at that. It's also about how I discovered that Mass, not Time, is the next variable in retrocausality.

First off, I'm sitting in the pew thinking how am I going to get through this, what with the kids climbing all over each other and making a racket on one side of me and the fat guy making all kinds of slurping and licking sounds like he was about to eat me on the other, and Fr. Szemeredi having the entire week off to go to some Eucharist convention (they have them?) so that we had this Indian priest with dark hair and thick glasses and an even thicker accent, and the guitar player out on vacation cause it's August now and everybody wants to go to the beach and drink beer and eat hot-dogs, and this girl from the Youth Group with the highest pitched voice I've ever heard doing the readings, which I never heard, and the sun coming through the eyeballs of a stained glass St. Margit burning up my arm, and the idea scratching at the back of my head that I won't make it out alive, so please, God, help me! I almost screamed, which I've been doing a lot of lately (it's not like I don't have a reason), but then I knew it would get back to mom big time, so I didn't. Here's what I did instead: I gave up. I mean, when you add it all up, I had nothing to really scream about. I had Laura, we finally kissed, I was about to go on a journey of not one but two thousand miles, and I was sitting on top of the world. So what did I care if I got stuck in a pew? No big deal. I'd just wait it out and ask for God's blessing again on the Great Escape. After all, you can't have too many blessings on an interstate kidnapping. You have to take the philosophical view, which is what Mr. Andrade always says. I guess I never knew that that meant till now.

So, I put my pen down, sat back, and looked at what was going on. And that's when it hit me: this thing they were doing up there was all about love and sacrifice and blood and betrayal and giving yourself over to someone so completely that you wanted to jump up and shout, "Sweet Jesus, come and be my everything, step into my life and penetrate my innermost being so that I am flush with ecstasy and joy and let me be your servant while you are my king to do with whatever you please. I am completely yours forever and ever. Amen!"

That's when I realized that Jesus Christ was none other than Laura Fedora! I mean, come on, that's exactly what I've been thinking and saying about her ever since I got this journal with the red cover. The very same thing using the same words, even. So, church, religion, and faith were somehow connected to love, sex, and getting your body whipped into submission by a redhead. I just couldn't figure out *how* all of it was connected, so I sat there like a zombie, watching and listening to everything that Indian priest did, trying to figure out how church and the garage behind Laura's house fit together. It was a little scary, cause then I thought maybe *they were the same thing.* That was too much to bear, so I scribbled some notes on the bulletin to think about later, which made Fat Guy look over at me, but I didn't care. This was serious. And it got even more serious when the priest said the Eucharistic Prayer. Now I couldn't take my eyes off him.

"On the night he was <u>betrayed</u>, he took bread and gave you thanks and praise. He broke the bread, gave it to his disciples, and said: 'Take this, all of you, and eat it: this is my body which will be given up for you.'"[17]

How many times had I heard those same words, that same prayer, at the same altar every Sunday for years (okay, maybe not *every* Sunday, but let's not get technical when there's a major point to be made) and never really understood that Jesus was giving his disciples his *body* to eat? His body was a meal that was human and divine, body and soul, sexual and spiritual, and this meal was exactly what church was all about. And since the meal was himself, a sacrifice of himself, that meant that the connection of church to garage was through Jesus. And not just any old part of Jesus but his death. So, *ipso facto*, faith and sex were connected through death. You had to die to really understand both. Well, what do you know about that? If that wasn't the craziest but best news in the entire world, what was? Laura could shoot me a hundred times for all I cared, cause it wouldn't be about her killing me but about sex and love and—

Oh, my God, Christ's dying on the cross was about Sex...!

Just as I thought this, the altar boy hit the Golden Gong three times with his black rubber mallet, which somehow got me so stiff it hurt, and by the time the echo of the third hit faded, the Dirty Deed (Seed) was done. The church was so quiet and my senses so raw I thought I could actually hear myself come in my pants. I guess I had worked myself up so much that the mother next to me thought I was overcome with love of Jesus, so she handed over a Kleenex, which was passed down the line of fourteen kids until it got to me. I nodded in her direction and then wiped the sweat from my face. I was so humiliated, I cried right then and there. I was exhausted and shaking. I buried my face in

---

17 *I underlined the important parts and will go back over the writing with my red pencil.*

my hands, trying to hide, and looked down to see if there was a stain on my pants, but it was dry. Thank God nobody, not even the ushers taking up the collection with their baskets on a stick, bothered me. They must have thought I was so deep in prayer that I was sweating blood, which wouldn't have surprised me. I'm glad I couldn't see myself kneeling there like a pathetic blob of wet underwear. This made my obsession with feet about as bad as preferring the strawberry strip in spumoni to the chocolate or vanilla one: something you don't usually see, but nothing you couldn't tell the old ladies selling baklava in the basement about.

Anyway, that's what happened, and I stayed in the pew through three rounds of "Now Thank We All Our God," which was painful. I don't know if I am going to hell or not, but I do know that Mass is a wonderful thing, more important than Distance, Time, and Speed, all of which have turned out to be imposters of physics compared to the experience of coming in church. Honestly, I never thought I'd say anything like that, and I don't know if it will ever happen again. I hope not. Everything was aligned just right for it this time, so what are the odds? I guess I won't have a chance to really think about what happened, cause once it's over, it's over. It's also too embarrassing to keep writing about. Let this be the only record of it. I did my job, wrote about it, tried to figure it out like a real writer, and am leaving it with you, the reader, to do whatever you want with it. Hopefully, I'll be long gone and you'll have mercy on my children, especially the strange ones like me. There, that's an end of it.

Wednesday, August 11
"If love be rough with you, be rough with love!"…Dude…

Wednesday's the easiest day of the week because the sports schedule is already posted, so you know which group of kids is doing what, with the younger kids playing kickball and Wiffle ball and stuff like that and the older kids doing their thing with volleyball, softball, and basketball. Frisbee's big, too, but I find it annoying, even after the other day. So I hung out with Lindeman for a while, but all he was interested in was finding out if Laura and I "did it" up at Valley Forge. He can be a jerk sometimes. Besides, I didn't want to stand around in the sun all that time, so I went to the portables to talk to Mr. Andrade about you know what. He wasn't there, but guess what? I found him in the faculty parking lot under the hood of his car. The canvas cover was rolled up neatly past the windshield onto the roof. It was now or never.

"Hey, Mister Andrade," I said, coming up to him as he leaned over the engine adjusting the distributor cap. A brown, rusted toolbox lay on the ground next to him.

"How now, Mercurio! How goes it, fair youth?"

Here we go again.

"Very well, sir, and you?"

He looked up at me and smiled.

"Would that the stars shine as favorably on thy house as they have on mine own."

"For that, my lord, I can only be but glad."

"And I am gladder still that thou hast a glad butt."

"Sir?"

He laughed. "In truth, I warrant thou didst not come here to tell a tale of butts but of something higher."

"'Indeed, 'tis true, for I have other desires."

"Then come, speak plainly, and let thy words hold mine ears captive."

I stood there, not sure what to say, since I had just about gone through my Globe Theatre repertoire.

"I bid thee speak," he said. "Or dost thou find thyself in a pickle?"

"Indeed, a veritable pickle, in a manner of speaking."

"And what manner is that?"

"Both sweet and sour, sir."

At that, he burst out laughing, slammed the hood down, and shook his head. Then he wiped sweat from his face and leaned back against the dented blue fender of the—oh, my God, *Mercury Comet!* The word "Comet" was in chrome lettering on the lower part of the fender, shining in the sun as if it were speaking to me. And it *was* speaking to me: TAKE THE GIRL TO WYOMING, TAKE THE GIRL TO WYOMING!"

"If I might make bold, Mercurio, perchance is the depth of thy sweet and sour affection measured out in ginger curl and temper?"

"Ginger?"

"I speak of the redheaded maiden of the 'Chateau of Chapeau.'"

I must have looked really stumped, because he followed up right away with, "The Fedora girl."

"You have hit the mark," I said.

"And 'tis clear as day that thou hast not, but, alas, the course of true love never did run smooth."

He started unraveling the cover back down the windshield, so I went to the other side to help.

"How might I help thee?" he said at last.

"A horse, a horse, my kingdom for a horse!"

Pretty lame, I know, but I couldn't think of anything else. I was desperate. He stopped, looked at me, and said, "Well, thou art Richard. I pray thee, proceed."

"No, truly, sir, I need a horse."

"A horse? Why, hast thy love galloped away?"

"Nay, a horse in a manner of speaking."

"What manner of man is this that hath yet another manner of speaking? And what manner be it this time?"

"A wagon."

"Wagon?"

"Aye, sir."

I tapped the hood just as I covered the front grill. Then I stood up and explained in my best Elizabethan English: "In two night's time a concert is to be given by the very same musicians that have forged the arrow in Cupid's bow. They are Aerosmith, the favorite band of my love, Laura, who lavishes her complete devotion upon them.[18] I have come hither in the hope that you might grant my wish of conveying her to the concert in this fiery Comet."

"I see," he said, thinking it over. "Knowest thou this, Mercurio. Any other youth would have received my reply anon, but since there is so much to commend in thee, answer three questions and the Comet will whisk thee and thy love to the gates of paradise. It remains but for thee to open them."

"And should I fail?"

"Thy kingdom shall be mine."

"My kingdom?"

"For a horse, recountest?"

"The terms are dear."

"But the dear tender. What sayest thou?"

I exhaled. "Ready, sir."

He cleared his throat and said in a voice as phony as a TV game show host's, "Question, the first—uh, these are mostly fill-in, Mercurio—[*more throat-clearing*]...Two households, both alike in—?"

It was from *Romeo and Juliet*. I remembered the word, because it had never made much sense to me.

"Dignity."

"Correct. Here follows question, the second: The fault, dear Brutus, lies not in the stars but in—?"

"Ourselves."

"Well played, Mercurio, well played. And now, the third and final question, playing for the 1964 Mercury Comet, ladies and gentlemen, in the form of an essay..."

---

18 *Why, I know not.*

"Essay?"

"I did say *mostly.*"

He paused here, and I wasn't sure if he was trying to come up with something or was just adding to the drama.

"How dost thou study a woman?"

"What?!?"

He repeated the question. This wasn't an essay, multiple choice, multiple answer, matching, or scratch-n-sniff. It was a riddle, a real riddle, and the answer probably wouldn't be found in some scene from *Titus Andronicus.* I would actually have to think about it. So I shifted my weight a bunch of times and thought about it. I came up with nothing. I shifted some more and came up with more nothing. This wasn't looking good. How do you study a woman? With a textbook? Magnifying glass? Microscope? Slide rule? No, not a slide rule. That's how they would study us. Protractor? Maybe, but did I want to use up my answer on that? I raised my hand.

"Yes?"

"How many guesses?"

"Art thou a cat?" he asked.

I shook my head.

"Alas, but one."

"Clues?"

"Aye, here's one: Rodrigue, as-tu du coeur?"

Oh, my God, he was quoting something from French literature! I didn't recognize it. How could I? We were only on *Parlez-Vous: Livre Trois* for cryin out loud! And who the hell was Rodrigue, anyway? This wasn't *faire*...! None of it was...I started to panic. Then I started resenting the whole stupid business with Elizabethan English. Why did I agree to this? I pictured having to ride the bus down to the Spectrum Friday night. How ridiculous would that be? And what was I supposed to do after, hitchhike with Laura all the way to Wyoming?

"You are too hard for me, sir," I told him.

I turned and walked away. I could tell he was watching me, but then he went back to collecting his tools and things without saying anything. I was hoping for a "Hey, Richard, wait. I was just kidding. You can have the car, and here's twenty bucks. Go have yourself a good time." But it didn't happen. I knew it wouldn't happen. Things didn't work that way, and I'm not sure I wanted them to.

When I got to the fence separating faculty parking from the portables, I stopped. I couldn't believe this was happening. What about all the stuff I had been through: the plotting, the trees, Valley Forge, Norm, dad, all that crossing your heart business, "I love you," one omen after another like they were hotcakes (mom's saying), this is my body, and now a Mercury Comet with chrome lettering? What the hell was all that for? What was the point of it? Nothing, that's what. It all added up to a Big Fat Zero, Zilch, Goose Egg. How could you have all those things pointing in one direction like some raging river only for them to be wrong and meaningless? Did that whole thing with the freakin penguins even mean anything? I tortured myself over it. Still do. Now I find out that penguins are just birds on prom night, except they can't fly and that's that. So shut up and take a seat, Mercurio.

Haec avis non volare potest.[19]

I reached the Day Camp in a daze. What did this mean about Laura, then? I had given her my heart, and now that heart really was shot through. Okay, not by her, which at least would have been romantic, but by not getting some stupid riddle right. I had failed, lost the game, swing-and-a-miss, strike three. The fault lies not in the stars but in me. *Richard, as-tu du coeur*—do you have *heart?* The answer was no, not anymore. I had no heart, and from that moment on nothing would ever be the same. I looked up and saw the pool and lifeguard stand with Tommy twirling his whistle around his fingers. I saw the sycamore tree with the picnic tables

---

19 *"This bird can't fly," which means my plot as much as penguins. In fact, my plot could be a penguin: stupid to look at and completely useless for flying. Was it good for anything? Yeah, for wasting my time, from scheming to road maps to tree houses. I guess it made time stand still for me. I should tell dad about it. I invented a time machine!*

below. I saw the gym and Girls and Boys Bathrooms and Animal Habitat, where Squiggly and Piggly were running around snorting and crapping up a storm. It was all there, right in front of me, but none of it was the same. It was like they were as fake as the *Oklahoma!* backdrop. And then somehow—I have no idea how, since it happened just as I let a sliver of spit drop into the dust—I realized that the answer to the riddle was right in front of me, too. It was there the whole time.

Rodrigue, as-tu du coeur?

In the time it took me to tear back to faculty parking, I broke a sweat. Mr. Andrade was at the door of his office.

"Is it too late?" I screamed.

He turned around and covered his eyes to see who it was. Then he put his rusted toolbox down.

"No, you never used up your guess," he said.

"Then my answer to the third and final question is—"

This time, *I* waited for dramatic effect.

"Yes?"

"By heart. The way you study a woman is by heart!"

He got this huge grin on his face, picked up the toolbox, and said, "Come and fetch thy keys, Mercurio. Thy chariot awaits."

Thursday, August 12

Okay, so at first I was really pumped—I mean, who wouldn't be, right? I had snatched victory from the jaws of Lady Macbeth, but then it felt like I was stabbing Mr. Andrade in the back again. *Et tu, Brute?* He had been so nice to me—trusted me even—that I must be a louse to steal his Comet. Sure, I could pay him back, but even if I did, would I ever be able to look him in the eye again? And the funny thing about it is, fate is on my side—there's no question about it—but I still have to betray a teacher I admire and respect. Is that Meant-to-Be, too?

I was thinking about all this cleaning up the gym at the end of the day. The kids are supposed to do it, put the balls and games away, but they never do it right and there's always something missing or broken. So, I was sitting on the floor collecting loose marbles (!) when I looked up to see somebody standing in the doorway. I couldn't make them out right away because of the light, but then whoever it was came closer and I saw that it was Laura. There was a halo of light shining behind her and her hair hung down around her shoulders and her legs flowed into her sandaled feet with those toes that would have made it hard for me to see anything else even without the glare. She wore ragged cutoffs with straw sandals and a green halter top that matched her eyes and dark lipstick that matched her toenails. I stared at her and the only thing I could think of was kissing her again. There's just something about the second time. The first is the first and there's no beating it, cause look at all the trees I had to go through to get to that sweet sassafras. *Ass-a-frass.* The waiting almost killed me. And the third time (I haven't had it yet, so I'm just guessing) is already something you expect. It's like, sure, we're official so we kiss all the time. No big deal. But the Second Kiss is special. See, you've already cleared the hurdles. You've got the girl and everything's great for the time being. And it's *for the time being* that's awful, cause what if it doesn't happen again, what if she changes her mind, what if it was a mistake, what if it wasn't Meant-to-Be? You don't really know. It's like you've tasted coconut custard pie for the first time and you're dying to have more, but you don't know if you'll ever be able to have it again. It's that second slice, when they finally serve it, that makes all the difference.

"So, what are you doing?" she asked, coming toward me. I shot up and sent a bunch of marbles rolling across the floor like ball bearings.

"Looks like you're losing your marbles," she said, giggling.

I stood there.

"So, where have you been?" she asked.

"Been?"

"I haven't heard from you since Saturday."

"Oh, I called a couple times, but I kept getting nonno."

She looked at me, not exactly suspicious but not too trusting, either.

"You haven't changed your mind, have you?"

"About what?"

She gave me a look.

"God no, Laura. It's just that..."

"What?"

"Well, I've been trying to get ready for the concert tomorrow night, you know, being prepared."

"Prepared?"

"Like a ride. I know you want to go with your brother, but I asked Mister Andrade, and he said we could borrow his car."

"Really?"

"Yeah, the old one he keeps at school in faculty parking."

"Cool."

"You're not mad, then?"

"No, I think it's kinda sexy, us going to the concert alone. I'll just tell Enz we'll meet them there."

"Great," I said, relieved.

She helped me scoop up the marbles and put the other stuff away. She put a game of Parcheesi on the top shelf of the storage closet, but she couldn't quite reach and had to stretch all the way from her tippy toes to her derriere, shoulder blades, neck, and fingertips. From behind, it was like watching her shoot from the foul line, except it wasn't like that at all. See my drawing of "Foul Line Laura."

"So, are you off now?" she asked, coming back down.

"Huh?"

"Are you off now?"

"I have to sign out."

"You don't have to go home?"

"I don't think so."

"You're not sure?"

"I'm sure, I think."

She stared at me, her eyes cat-like in the dull light of the closet. Would this be a good time to kiss her?

"Good, cause I thought we could go somewhere," she said.

"Really, where?"

"I have a place in mind. It's a surprise. I love surprises."

"Me, too," I said.

I hate surprises. People think they're doing you a favor by surprising you with something or other that turns out to be lame, stupid, or completely unrelated to anything in your life. Like the time Aunt Kitti brought me a wool hunting cap from Hungary with fluffy, white ear flaps. "You look so handsome, Ri—chard," she told me as she pressed her bulbous breasts into my face and smeared my cheek with lipstick.

After signing out and Mr. Andrade reminding me not to forget to lock the gate to the faculty parking lot when we get back from the concert tomorrow night (thank God he was busy with some parents and didn't have time to talk), Laura took me by the hand. We crossed Washington, went down 13th, and turned right onto Ellsworth, which was the opposite direction from her house.

"Where are we going?"

"You'll see."

We walked down Ellsworth, hung a left on Broad, and before I knew it we were standing across the street from the St. Rita of Cascia Shrine. It was this gray granite slab with columns and a dark wooden door and gold cross. It looked like a mausoleum. I thought of *The Omen* and looked up to see if there were any lightning rods on the roof. It looked safe. Still, I didn't know what to say.

"What do you think, Merk?"

"I don't know what to say."

"But you understand, don't you? I have to go in and I didn't want to go alone."

"Absolutely," I said, holding her hand up to my mouth and kissing her fingers.

We crossed the street and went up the steps to the wooden doors. It was dark and cool inside, which was nice after the walk. It looked like all the other churches I'd been in: huge pillars, stained glass (this one had the life of St. Rita), flickering candles, pews, Stations of the Cross, pink-colored walls (that was a little different), statues, a big organ with gold pipes in the choir loft, a white marble altar and tabernacle, and marble statues of angels on either side of the altar with the tips of their wings crossed. That was different, too, hadn't seen that anywhere else. At least it was quiet. There were four or five other people there, mainly old. I wanted to hang back, but Laura went up to the communion rail and knelt down to pray. I followed her as far as the third pew and sat down. When she came back, I moved over.

"Thanks for coming," she said.

"Sure."

"I made an appointment with Father Jim. I want to see if he remembers my mother coming here."

"Who's Father Jim?"

"The pastor. He sounded very nice on the phone."

"Laura, how do you know he was even here back then? Wasn't it like twelve years ago or something?"

"I just want to talk to somebody."

"How about your mother?"

She looked down.

"I can't talk to her. She won't tell me the truth. She hates my dad."

"I thought she hated nonno."

"She hates him, too, but only because he's my dad's father. Well, that and he breaks things."

"So why don't you talk to your dad?"

"You don't understand," she said. "My family's not like yours."

"Hey, I wouldn't complain if I were you."

"What do you mean?"

"Your family may be loud, mean, and nasty, but at least you've got money to do things and they take care of each other."

She looked at me a little funny, not nice funny but like the first time we met funny.

"Loud, mean, and nasty?" she said.

"Well, just that they're nasty to each other."

"And loud? What, cause we're Italian?"

"No, I didn't mean it like that."

"Like what, then?"

I moved closer and put my hand on her thigh. Then—I'm not sure why I did it and I'm beginning to think churches do to me what trees do to her (!)—I flashed my eyebrows, tilted my head to one side, and smiled.

"Wipe that smirk off your face," she said.

"That's just what Missus Miller used to say."

"Who's Missus Miller?"

"My fifth grade teacher. I'd always get in trouble and she'd say to me, 'Richard, wipe that smirk off your face!'"

"That's funny."

"What's funny?"

"You're the Merk with the Smirk."

"Been like that all my life."

"Interesting."

"Got me in a lot of trouble."

"I bet."

Then Fr. Jim came over, a big Irish-looking guy with an even bigger smile and red jowls that wiggled when he leaned over the pew and peered into the depths of your soul. He did it to Laura first, staring down at her breasts, and then me. He didn't seem to notice my breasts.

"Are you Laura by any chance?"

"Yes, I am. Father Jim?"

"That's me. So nice of you to come, Laura. I'm glad you called, and I'd be happy to talk to you. Now, who might this young man be?"

I was hoping he wasn't going to break into Elizabethan English. I'd had enough of that. Of course, it'd probably be Latin, not English. Now, that I could handle.

"Hello, Father. My name's Richard. I'm Laura's *boyfriend.*"

Yes, I did. I really did. I said the word, owned it, took possession of it like nobody's business. I don't know what made me do it, but it surprised both of them.

"I see," he said, straightening up. "Well, very happy to meet you as well, Richard." He put his hand out to shake, and it was soft and gooey.

"Laura, would you like to talk here or in my office?"

"Here's fine, I guess."

"All right, then. Richard, we have a nice gift shop and book-store downstairs. Why don't you see if anything interests you?"

"Yes, Father."

Yes, father, no, father, I don't know, father, sure thing, father, as you wish, father, kiss my heinie, father. There was something about the guy I didn't like right off the bat. He was too nice, for one. I don't know if it was phony or not, but I also didn't like the fact that he snuck up on us like Lindeman in the locker room. It was really strange, a guy that big coming out of nowhere like that. But I was happy to get away from yet another crime scene. The nave, I mean (any nave). There I was, a knave in the nave (hah—get it?). I was pretty sure I wasn't going to find anything worthwhile in Ye Ole Gift Shop, but I went anyway, figuring I'd give Laura as much time as she needed. So I trudged down this old staircase with an iron railing and plaster peeling off the walls to the basement, where I heard music. By the way, I don't know what's going on, but I've had my fair share of churches, basements, strange music, and old people lately. It's not that I don't like old people and their music. I just don't understand them. Maybe I will but not now. I also have this theory about age, and this is as good a time to tell it as any, since I followed the music wafting from the gift shop and stood outside the glass partition, lis-tening to this French woman sing and watching another old woman well over four feet put Mass cards into a wire display rack.

So, here's my theory. I call it "The Theory of Peaking" and it goes like this: you are what you are, say, a runner or teacher or singer or ballplayer or priest or used car salesman or even a "renowned Goschenhoppen historian," and the thing that makes you any of these—your *penguinity*, let's call it—peaks at a certain time and then fades away. *Exempli gratia*: Shirley Temple peaked at the age of six or eight or whatever when she was singing about lollipops, and then faded away (the ambassador stuff I'm counting as a by-product of her childhood stardom). Then there's a guy like Tiny Tim who peaked as an adult playing a ukulele and tip-toeing through the tulips, until he, too, faded away. Finally, there's George Burns who, even though was in radio and television for like a century-and-a-half, peaked as an old man and even played in a movie with that guy from *The Odd Couple*. So, no matter what we end up doing for a living, each of us has a time when we peak, when our *penguinity* blossoms. For some, it's early, others mid-life, and still others old age. It's our *Penguinity Index* (I call it "PI"). I've already determined that mine is high, so I will peak during old age. I'm a George Burns type of guy, which means (1) I am not about to die no matter what mom says, and (2) I am going to figure out old people when I become one, not before. All of which is a long way of saying that I had no idea what the woman with the Mass cards was trying to say to me when she came over, waving a St. Rita card in front of my face.

"I'm sorry, what?"

"La Vie en Rose, do you like it?"

"O, j'adore," I said, which is really not good to do, because then people think you're a Frenchy.

Sure enough, the woman started rattling off in French, which I can't seem to get away from, and it occurred to me that she might be from Montreal, which meant I could never tell Norm.

"It's Edith Piaf," she said finally *en anglais*, "singing one of the most romantic songs ever written."

"Romantic?"

"Mais oui, mon ami."

"But we're in church."

She smiled, took me by the hand, and—*Aide, Mme Dudoit!*—started dancing with me, singing along to the record: *Quand il me prend dans ses bras, il me parle tout bas...*blah...blah, blah, blah, blah, blah...blaaah...blah, blah, blah, blah, blah...blaaah...*etc., etc...*

When we finished I looked around to make sure nobody was watching. If it ever got out that I was—

"Say, can you write the words down for me?" I asked. "I mean, I study French in school but I couldn't follow what she was saying."

"Of course, dear. But you need the practice, not me," she said, showing me the album and handing me a pad and pen.

"Oh, right."

"A propos, je suis Josephine," she added, putting out her hand.

"Enchanté. I am Ree—chard," I said, taking her hand.

"Well, Ree—chard, you need practice dancing, too."

"I know."

"So, shall we?"

Before I could say anything, she put the record back on and we took up our "position."

"What position?"

"Dance position. Ready? Comme ça...un-deux-trois, step, un-deux-trois, step...feel the rhythm. But you have to go this way, not that. Oui, c'est vrai....un-deux-trois, step, un-deux-trois... Now there...that's right, now here...oui...Don't stare at your feet. Ah, but don't step on mine!"

"Sorry."

"...un-deux-trois, step, un-deux-trois, step..."

We danced around the room (twirled, really), which was hard to do stooped over with all my weight on my toes, but after a while I was getting the hang of it and didn't feel so bad. Then Edith hit the high note at "...*pour la veeeeeee—a...!*" and I got so excited (I was a little dizzy from the twirling) that I backed into the wire rack with all the Mass cards, knocking it over and making the record skip. Then I stepped on Josephine's foot, and she yelled something in French that didn't sound at all like *mots d'amour*.

"Well, I think that's enough for now," she gasped with tears in her eyes.

"Here, let me help you clean up."

"That's very kind of you, Richard, but no need. I'm sure you must have homework or something to do."

"It's August."

"Yes, well I just need to sit down for a minute," she said, ignoring me and hobbling away to the Ladies Room.

I stood there in the middle of the mess with the needle making a thumping sound over and over as it hit the record label. It sounded like a windshield wiper. The rose color had faded, I guess. When it was obvious that Josephine wasn't coming back anytime soon, I started picking up the cards.

"What are you doing?" Laura said unexpectedly from the doorway. She was starting to ask me that a lot.

I looked up, glad to see her. "Who me?"

"No, the other guy."

"We had a little accident, that's all. Help me clean up and let's get out of here!"

"We?"

I shrugged. "It's a long story. Come on."

We picked up the rack, put the cards in some sort of order, and turned off the record player. Then we raced up the stairs and out the front door to the street.

"So did you talk to the priest?" I asked once we were a safe distance away.

She nodded.

"Did it help?"

"A little. You were right. He wasn't there when we were, but he had some nice things to say."

"Like what?"

"You know, the usual stuff about marriage and how hard it is and that Saint Rita's example is one of forgiveness even when you want to kill your husband."

"Seriously, he said that?"

"No, I added that, but that's what it was about. Oh, and how my mother still loves me and that I should talk to her—just what you said."

"So, are you going to?"

"No."

I looked at her. "You're stubborn, you know that?"

She didn't say anything, which for Laura meant only one thing: I was right. And I knew I was right. I've known her long enough to know there's only one thing that stops her dead in her tracks: the truth. She can't beat it, nobody can. So, why bother? She didn't say a word the entire time we walked down Broad Street, this time toward Wharton.

"We going to the park?" I asked, taking her hand. It was the first time I felt sorry for her, not because she had this thing going on at home but because I had beaten her fair and square. It was the first time that happened. Who knew, maybe there were other firsts in store for me, especially tomorrow night.

"Nope."

"Then where?"

"My house. Nobody's home. We'll have the whole place to ourselves for at least an hour."

I didn't say anything, just looked at her without making it too obvious that this was the best day of my life. So maybe this was my surprise, my *real* surprise! I couldn't believe it. Stay cool, Merk, stay cool. See, all you have to do is never give up, persevere, and in the end you'll get what you want. It's a beautiful thing, really. I decided to go for broke.

"You know, Laura..."

"Yeah?"

"I've always wanted to see your garage, I mean what's in it and all. Would you show it to me?"

She kept walking, holding my hand, looking down at the cracks in the sidewalk as we passed over them (I avoided them, just like the staircase at home). She didn't ask why, didn't say how ridiculous it was or that I was a pervert, didn't stop and look at me sideways.

"Sure, I'll show you whatever you want."

I'll show you whatever you want. All my dreams were coming true! I don't know what I did to deserve this, especially after crippling Josephine, but this was the greatest Meant-to-Be of all time, me and Laura Fedora with her red hair and halter top and toes of pure acrylic and breasts that made me tremble and shake. In that garage next to the mimosa tree with the dilapidated roof and broken window I will have my second serving of coconut custard pie. Yes, I will! Thank you, God!

When we got to her house with the cherry tree and "F" on the door, she did something strange. Instead of going into the house and through the kitchen to the yard, which is what we usually do, she led me down the side where there was an old wooden gate with a huge padlock that looked like a prop from *Treasure Island.* She undid the lock, which wasn't locked, anyway, and we walked down a cement path lined with zucchini and cucumbers and other things, eggplant maybe, and grape vines (I had no idea any of this was there) to the yard and then from there to the garage. It was like a secret entrance. And all the time she didn't say a word, didn't even look at me. She just kept her head down and her eyes on the ground, which was about the strangest thing I've ever seen her do. It was like she was hiding from something.

The garage had two wooden doors that swing out. She tugged on one, which opened with a long drawl and came to rest just wide enough for us to squeeze through without touching. Inside was perfectly still and looked like the hull of a ship with wooden beams and rafters and studs. The pointed ends of rusted nails stuck out all over the walls so that if you got too close, it'd be tetanus, for sure. There was a workbench with tools spread out on the far side of the garage, and closer to us were a car engine on a mount, wire manikins, unlabeled wine bottles in racks, and a swivel chair on casters with a flat seat and spindle back. Some of the spindles were missing. Cobwebs were all over the place, and a broken floor mirror stood leaning against the wall behind the chair. The place was cool and smelled of gasoline, not a lot, just enough to give you a romantic buzz. At least I had one. I don't know about Laura.

"Well, here it is," she said, looking around. "What did you want to see, exactly?"

"You," I said.

She smiled. "I don't have hair on my chest, if that's what you're worried about."

"I didn't think you did."

"And I'm not showing it to you."

I went up and put my arms around her. Her eyes were darker, almost blending with the wood around us as if she were a chameleon. I parted her hair from her face and moved in for the Second Kiss, the smell of gasoline like champagne to me.

"Do you love me, Merk?" she asked, tilting her head back.

"Of course I do, you know it."

"What do you love about me?"

Dangerous territory, this. Even I knew that. When a girl asks you that question, she has a particular answer in mind. It's not an essay question or multiple choice but right or wrong. And, unlike Mr. Andrade's quiz, this one was a matter of life or death, thumbs up or down, my sexual coming of age or early retirement. Forget the Theory of Peaking, because there would be no peaking at all if I answered it wrong.

"Lots of things," I said.

"Such as?"

"You're a good writer and have great ideas for *The Review*."

"Really?"

"Sure."

"Go on."

"You're willing to run away with me just like that without worrying about how we'll do it or where we'll go."

"I think that's the man's job," she said.

"Exactly, which is why I have a plan."

"You do?"

"I call it the Great Escape."

"So tell me."

"Nope."

"Why not?"

"It's a surprise. You like surprises, right? So, I'll tell you tomorrow night at the concert."

"But I want to hear it now," she said, pushing me.

"No."

"Yes."

"No."

"Yes."

This time, she poked me with each "yes" until I landed on the seat of the chair, where she trapped me. She sat on my lap, her legs dangling to one side, her hand clutching my shirt. She was lighter than I thought, and I swear I could smell her sweat, which was incredible. She had the faintest touch of it on her legs, which were warm and sticky.

"Tell me," she whispered so close I could taste her breath.

"Not until tomorrow night, but I'll tell you a secret nobody else knows and is another reason I love you."

"Okay."

"Ready?"

"Yeah."

I slid my hand down her leg to her ankle and lifted her foot. The sandal was a slip-on, so I pushed it off and ran my fingers along the arch of her foot, then played with her polished toes. I was so tense and the garage was so still that I could hear wood cracking in the heat. I was barely breathing. I thought I heard a spider slide down a web.

"What are you doing?"

"Your feet, Laura, are the most beautiful things I've ever seen."

She looked at me puzzled and then something flashed across her face. I wasn't sure what it was until she burst out laughing. Then she jumped up and pointed at me.

"Why, you little pervert! You've been checking out my feet the entire time, haven't you?"

Fourth time stuttering.

"At the restaurant when you dove under the table—that wasn't a napkin. It was my feet you were checking out, wasn't it?"

More stuttering.

"Unbelievable! All this time you've been looking at my feet when I thought you were checking out my behind."

"Well, I was doing that, too."

"You were?"

"Sure, I mean—"

"Back at the Day Camp?"

I nodded.

"That's a relief," she said, staring at me.

"It is?"

"What do you think, Merk?"

"I dunno."

Really, I didn't. How was lusting after her plum better than obsessing over her beautifully shaped toes? God, were they beautiful! What would I do if she couldn't accept my obsession, my little *secret*? She kept staring at me without saying anything. Dust drifted through a shaft of sunlight between us. Then it got quiet, dirt quiet, without any sound from outside seeping in, not even traffic. Finally, she came close and whispered, "Take off your shirt."

"What?"

"Do it."

The girl doesn't mince words. I obeyed. She put her naked foot on the chair between my legs and nudged the chair toward the mirror. Then she moved her foot up to my chest and rested it there. I was on fire. Total, consuming fire.

"I can't hold it, Merk," she said after a while, trying to keep her balance.

I tried to hold her steady, but she started hopping around on one foot and had to drop the other one from my chest. Then she leaned in, grabbing both arms of the chair, and kissed me. Her lips were hot and moist and a few strands of her hair got caught between us. I didn't mind, though, and she wasn't embarrassed. It was like she wanted me and didn't care how things looked. There we were in her garage just as I had imagined, and I could practically hear the Starland Vocal Band strumming away in the corner.

She sat down on my lap again, holding me, one foot sandaled, the other bare.

"Do you love me, Merk?"

"Of course I do, you know it."

"Why?"

"Lots of reasons."

"Like what?"

I didn't answer. I patted her hair and watched our reflection in the broken mirror as we sat there holding each other. That was all she really wanted and all I really wanted, too. Life was sweet. Like fresh corn on the cob on a hot day. I didn't have a care in the world.

Friday, August 13
BLACK FRIDAY

NORM WAS RIGHT. He was. I don't know why it happened, not after everything we've been through, but tonight was a disaster. It was worse than a disaster. My life is over and I might as well commit myself to an old folks' home, tell them about the whole George Burns thing, except nothing will happen when I turn 100, *if* I turn 100. I'll be the same as I am now: miserable, destroyed, annihilated, a non-existent piece of excrement. The Raven's Turd has had the last laugh. Laura dropped a turd on me!

I'm writing this after midnight, so technically it's Saturday, August 14th, but I wanted to record it now so I'll remember the date forever, not that I'll ever forget it. It's like Pearl Harbor, a day of infamy. I don't even know where to begin, since my normal *disciplina romana* has up and died, caught the last train for the Coast like the Father, Son, and Holy Ghost. I'm not joking, either. Everybody else is asleep and I have the entire night to sit here and rack my brain over what happened at the concert, except why would I do that when the answer is obvious? Laura is crazy, plain and simple. The red hair and crazy eye should have been a dead giveaway. No way was she ever going to change. What made me think she would? Why didn't I listen to dad? Maybe I'm to blame for doing what I did and reacting that way, but—my God!—Bobby Fiore? Of all the things that could have happened tonight and all the ways it could have played out, it had to go that way, *Bobby Fiore?* Mr. GTO Chest Hair versus Mr. Late Bloomer Borrowed Comet? After all the thinking and wondering and going back and forth like a rocking chair about tonight, it really comes down to one word—BETRAYAL—which I find more than a little ironic, considering this was the girl who cried on my shoulder about her father's hanky-panky and how betrayal was the worst thing that could happen to a person. Well, it happened to me and I can tell you she's right. Like father like daughter, I guess. Now that my eyes are open, I see it everywhere. *Perfidia Ubique Est.* And I have all night to think about my miserable, stupid life, maybe even all day tomorrow and all year at school, too. Should I quit *The Review*? Why would I stay? It'd be torture, screw the football team. I'm really confused.

All right, I had to do something, so I went ahead and did it. I feel better now and have a new appreciation for the Greek word *gymnos*, which means "naked" and is where we get our word "gymnasium." I'll tell you what I did even though I'm getting ahead of myself. Besides, it's not half as bad as what happened at St. Stephen's, and I feel a professional responsibility to divulge everything, although without drawings this time. I am also recording the events in this journal for posterity, assuming there is a posterity and they want to read about their ancestor whose life fell apart because of a Redheaded Vixen. I mean, what I did isn't so bad and even got me thinking about things in general, you know, the bigger picture and the meaning of life and all. Right, like there is one. I'm going to have a serious talk with Fr. Szemeredi first chance I get. Just when I open up and tell the girl of my dreams that I love her and even think of real reasons for loving her, not made up ones like we were destined for each other or are soulmates or any of that soupy crap they play on the Big 99, she crushes my heart, squeezes it until blood and tissue ooze from between her fingers like Chicken Ming gravy.

So, here it is. Speaking of the Big 99, I drove myself home from the concert in the rain listening to "Neither One of Us" by Gladys Knight & the Pips without Laura and without loading the Comet with the supplies I had hidden in the garage: sleeping bags; a cooler filled with drinks (plenty of Uncola for my un-beloved); blankets; a change of clothes; a shave kit with toiletries; jumper cables; two flashlights; plenty of Cheez-its, Raisinets, and Pecan Sandies; the road maps and Wyoming picture book from Norm; and the translation of "La Vie en Rose" (that's a joke!). I pulled the Comet into the driveway, went into the house, ran up the stairs without bothering about the distribution of weight, and plopped dead weight onto my bed. The frame rattled but nobody woke up. I lay there for a while, too tired to cry, otherwise I would have, but at least there hadn't been a lot of traffic and I had made it back to the house without skidding or getting pulled over. I guess I won't have to betray Mr. Andrade after all.

After a while—I don't know how long—maybe ten minutes, maybe forever, I got up and opened my closet to look at myself in the mirror hanging on the other side of the door. I felt awful, groggy. I couldn't breathe. My clothes burned my skin. So I got undressed, took everything off and left them in a pile at my feet: shirt, shoes, belt, pants, socks, underwear. Then I stood up straight and took a good, long look at myself. That's not something I've ever done before. Most of the time you want to get undressed and dressed again as fast as possible so nobody gets any ideas, especially in the locker room or during practice. So I never really bothered to look at myself like that, not even in the shower. I've been too afraid. I wasn't afraid now, though, so I looked. And what I saw was a boy, nothing else. A hairless, thin, pale body with a tinge of blue around the edges and a beaver-head of hair; bones and elbows and joints and a thick pubic finger that wasn't too interested in anything, even me staring at it. It didn't care at all. I got up closer to the mirror, exhaled on the glass and rubbed it till it squeaked. I lifted the hair off my forehead and inspected the welt from when Laura threw the Bic lighter at me and hit me square in the middle of the forehead. That's when something else hit me.

"Oh, my God!" I said out loud. "Saint Rita's wound of love!"

And it was. A wound of love that hurt just as much as any shot through my heart could have. I had no idea when we met at school today that things would turn out this way, that she would hurl the lighter at me in a fit of Red-Headed-Fedora-ness. Had no idea that Bobby Fiore would be there and that the day would become Black Friday. How could I? Who am I, Joyce Brothers? Kreskin? Carnac the Magnificent?

So, sitting naked at my desk and writing it all out till dawn (definitely <u>not</u> Dusk and Dawn), I can tell you exactly what happened.

Here it is:

I was in faculty parking next to the Comet when Laura walked up. She wore a short, pink skirt and a blue-striped blouse with yellow trim at the neck. She had a blue pocketbook that matched her blouse along with blue toenails and fingernails. Her sandals were yellow leather and, with the toenail polish and pink skirt, made me think of bubblegum and taffy. It was cool and I told her so.

"Thanks," she said.

"You kinda match the car."

She smiled.

"You ready?"

"For Aerosmith? Anytime."

"Great, let's do it!"

I opened the passenger door like a gentleman (always the freakin gentleman) and let her in, then went around to the driver's side. As I drove down South Broad I'd sneak a peek every once in a while at her feet, and by the time we got to Pattison she said, "You like my toenail polish?"

"Sure do."

"Maybe you can give me a foot massage later."

I swallowed and the car swerved. "Seriously?"

"Yeah."

"You don't think I'm a pervert?"

"Oh, I *know* you're a pervert. It's just that I don't think being a perv is so bad. Besides, I kinda like it."

I paid the parking attendant and drove to the north side of the Spectrum. I pulled into the spot where they told me, put the car in park, and turned off the key.

"What do you like about it, my being a perv, I mean?"

She shrugged. "The attention, I guess."

That was good enough for me. I leaned over and kissed her. She didn't resist this time and even looked like she enjoyed it. I liked the taste of her lipstick. Smooch Number Three.

"Come on, let's find Enz and Ronnie," she said.

Inside "The House that Rock Built" (there were posters), it was crazy. People were running around everywhere and there were long lines at the concession stands. Our tickets were in Section 113 on the 11th Street side, but first we had to look for Enz and Purple Head. We found them on the restaurant level at a concession stand behind the stage. Enz was dressed in jeans and a black vest, Ronnie had his usual undertaker outfit on, purple hair, and eyeliner. He was already stoned. I could see why Big Al had banned him from the house.

"Ronnie's got a friend in security who might be able to get us backstage passes," Enz said. "Wanna pretzel?"

"Wow, that's fantastic! Let us know for sure," Laura said. "No, I can't eat now. I'm too excited!"

"Merk?"

"Absolutely."

"What, you're not excited?"

"Every time I see you, Enz."

Luckily, he thought it was funny and bought me a pretzel. When I went for mustard, I saw a bunch of Laura's friends hanging out near a stairwell and giggling. It was the usual crowd except Big-Butt wasn't there and there was some other guy who didn't look too familiar until he turned around and I saw that it was Bobby Fiore with his World Famous Mustache. He was wearing a fringed suede jacket, which made me feel a little better, cause he looked like a moron. But then I got a sudden panic attack, cause what if the girls he was with actually thought he was cool? Where would that leave me?

"So, where are you guys?" I asked when I got back.

"Section 101, opposite you and Laura," Enz said. "After the concert, let's meet up backstage and we'll see about the passes."

"Okay."

"By the way, Merk..."

"Yeah?"

"Nice look."

Enz winked at me and then headed off, grinning, with Purple Head in tow.

"What was that about?"

"You've got mustard on your nose," Laura said.

Of course I did. The only question was what had stopped me from going over to talk to Laura's friends looking like that? Dumb luck, I guess. It would also have brought attention to Bobby Fiore, which was the last thing I wanted to do, which made what I did do even more bizarre. No, bizarre is too nice a word. It was stupid, just plain stupid and one of the biggest mistakes of my love life, which will never get off the ground, Mercurius Variable or not.

"You'll never guess who I just saw with your friends," I said, wiping my face.

"Who?"

"I can't say."

"What?"

"Bobby Fiore. He was talking to Flute Girl, you know, the one with braces who plays in the jazz band. She was with us up at Valley Forge. What's her name?"

"Where?"

"Over there."

Before I could turn back, Laura made a beeline to the stairwell. I can't say I was surprised. After all, I had told her as a kind of test, a pass-fail test. Unfortunately for me, she was failing miserably. Still, I didn't think she would be so obvious. I stood there watching her. Then I did the only thing a self-respecting guy in my situation could do: I ripped off another piece of pretzel, chewed it down, and threw away the rest.

"Bobby—*Bobby Fiore*—how ya doin?" I asked, going up to them and putting my arm around Laura. He looked at me like he just remembered he had a toothache.

"Everybody, this is Merk," Laura said. She didn't add "my boyfriend," or "we're official," or even "we're on a date." Nothing.

"We know him," a girl with bangs and a red-sequined blouse with puffy sleeves said. I recognized her from Civics class: Jennifer Lupine.[20]

There was this awkward silence, so I asked, "Did you guys all come together?"

A girl with Farrah Fawcett hair said, "As many as could fit into Bobby's GTO. There's a lot of room in the backseat!" They all laughed like it was the funniest thing ever.

"Bobby leaves for California next week, so he's having a big party," Laura said.

---

20 *"Jenny Benny Lupine / Gonna getcha Supine . . ."*

"In the backseat? Wow, it must be big."

"No, at his place. He's starting at UCLA and his parents want to give him a big sendoff."

I'd love to give him a big sendoff. I stared at him, glared really. He glared back. Laura moved away and put an arm around him and said, "He's a BMOC now, not a little high schooler. He probably won't even remember Saint Rita's once he starts hanging out with all those surfer girls. Isn't that right?"

"Oh, I dunno about that. How could I forget you?" he said, pressing his face to hers and squeezing her shoulder. They both giggled.

"So, you're coming, right? It's Wednesday night at my place."

"Why Wednesday?"

"I have to leave Friday morning."

"All right, I'll be there. How could I miss the best party of the summer?"

They smiled at each other like they had this secret world between them, and I felt like puking but didn't. I just stood there glaring.

"Hey, we better get going," Flute Girl said, and they started to move off herd-like, including Laura.

I cleared my throat.

"Laura, I think we're this way."

There was a final Parting-Is-Such-Sweet-Sorrow scene between her and Bobby, and then we started the long walk around the Spectrum to our section. I say it was long, but it wasn't the length that was the killer. It was the feeling of being stabbed in the back, of being betrayed by the person closest to you. The whole concert thing felt like a conspiracy that Laura had been hatching all this time. And for what? To see Bobby "BMOC" Fiore? She didn't need me to do that. She could have come to the concert with her friends or on her own, but that's what really got me. I could see her acting like that if she had a thing for the guy, but how could that be after yesterday? I still think she loves me. So, if she loves me, why the hell was she all over him like white on sour cream (it's Hungarian)? That just made it worse. She loves me but didn't think anything of flirting with the guy *right in front of me*. I'll tell you, if that's what she's like on the *inside*—a traitor—then I don't want her as my girlfriend. It would have been better if she had told me straight out that she loved the guy. That I could understand. This other thing was bullshit.

"So, how do you know Bobby?" I asked.

"You're kidding? Everybody knows him."

"Right, what was I thinking?"

"I dunno."

"He's a god."

She looked at me. "What's up with you?"

"Nothing, except what was all that 'best party of the summer' crap? Did you notice I wasn't invited, just you?"

"Of course you were."

"No, I wasn't. He never said a word to me."

"I'm sure he meant to. An invitation to me is an invitation to you."

"What, everybody knows that, too?"

She stopped on the last concrete step to our row.

"Are you jealous?"

"Nobody even knows we're together."

"What are you talking about?"

"You and him, that's what I'm talking about."

"You *are* jealous."

"No, I'm not."

"Yes, you are."

"No, I'm—"

I went up to the usher, who took my ticket and led me to my seat. Laura followed, and we sat set there without saying a word or even looking at each other. Then the band came on and went through their first set of songs, including "Sweet Emotion," "Dream On," and something about rats. I couldn't tell, though. I was too upset. As a matter of fact, I thought the whole concert was pretty stupid even though I sat there thumping my leg. Laura got into it big time, and soon a heavy haze of pot smoke hung over the crowd like a low-lying cloud. I have to admit it was pretty cool and I inhaled as much of it as I could. I think she caught me once, but really what did it matter? I thought about starting a life of drugs and crime. Why the heck not? It'd pay a lot more than Day Camp and be a cinch after all the lies and deceit with her. I even thought about starting at the concert by picking people's pockets. They were all stoned, anyway. They'd never know. It'd be gas money for the trip that we were probably not going to take anymore.

"So, are you going to talk to me?" I asked.

"I'm listening to the music."

"Yeah, so?"

"Look, Merk, I'm not the one with the problem. You are."

"Really, what's my problem?"

"You're obsessed with Bobby Fiore for some reason."

"What reason could that be?"

"I dunno. I haven't done anything."

"But you like him."

"No, I don't."

"Yeah, you do, don't deny it."

"That was a long time ago. We're just friends now."

"*What?*"

"Okay, so it was last year. I had a huge crush on him and he liked me. It ended and that's that."

"He liked you?"

She shrugged her shoulders, not taking her eyes off the stage as Steven Tyler climbed into what looked like a trapeze swing.

"So what the hell does that mean?" I asked.

"What does what mean?"

"Did you do it?"

As soon as I blurted it out, I realized how stupid it sounded. It was like I was Tommy or Kornél. She turned around and looked right at me.

"Are you crazy?"

"No, I'm not crazy. I saw how you flirted with him and thought—"

"What?"

"You know."

"No, tell me."

"You didn't answer my question," I said.

"Did I have sex with him?"

"Yes."

"How can you ask me that?"

"What else am I supposed to think?"

"I talk to the guy and get invited to his going-away party, and right away you think we had sex?"

"Ah, see, it was *you* he invited, not me!"

"You're impossible, you know that?"

"At least I'm not a liar and a cheat, and they're a lot worse!"

She stood up, grabbed her purse, and scooted out of the row past a bunch of rowdies just as they started playing "Walk This Way." I called after her but she wouldn't come back. I followed but tripped and almost went sprawling. I'm not sure it wasn't caused by somebody's foot. The usher caught me and set me back on my feet but not before everybody laughed. I caught up with her midway between the ramp and the restrooms.

"Where are you going?" I shouted.

"I have to go to the bathroom. Is that all right?"

"Look, I'm sorry I called you those things."

"No, you're not. You meant them."

"I was mad. I didn't know you went out with him. That was the first I heard of it."

"What's that got to do with anything?"

"Plenty. How can I trust you?"

"Who am I here with—you or him?"

I came this close to saying "whom" but decided not to.[21]
"Me," I said.

"All right, then."

"But you lied to me."

"I never lied to you. I just never told you everything."

Oh, so it was law school she was interested in, not journalism. Now I understood. The worst part is that she was absolutely serious, and I couldn't tell if she believed it or was just spreading more manure.

"So, are you telling me everything now?" I asked.

"I have to go to the bathroom, Merk."

She started to leave but I grabbed her arm.

"If you're here with me, what were you doing hanging all over him?"

"Leave me alone!"

"You did something with him, didn't you?"

She didn't answer.

"I knew it!"

"You know, you can be such a little boy."

"Really? Well a boy couldn't do what I planned to do after the concert tonight."

"What's that?"

"Forget it."

"Fine," she said, turning away to the music.

"—I was going to kidnap you and drive to Wyoming where we would both get jobs looking out for forest fires. I had it all worked out—maps, route, supplies, car, food, and you. A guy named Norm Fay helped me."

"Who the hell is Norm Fay?"

"Some guy I met."

"Some guy you met?"

"Yeah."

---

21 *"This close"* is like *"This cold."* See Footnote 9.

"And whose car?"

"The Comet."

"Mister Andrade's?"

"That's right."

"So, that's your 'Great Escape?'" she said, making quotation marks with her fingers (I hate it when people do that). "You were going to kidnap me and steal Mister Andrade's car so we could drive to Wyoming and live in the forest?"

"Well, when you put it that way, it sounds crazy, but I only did it so we could be together."

"You *are* crazy, then."

"For wanting to be with you?"

"No, for thinking that was the only way you could."

"That's what Norm said."

"Maybe he's right. We're here at the concert, aren't we?"

"It's not the same thing."

"What, cause you haven't kidnapped me yet? And what if I didn't want to go? What would you have done then?"

"I thought about it, but you told me you wanted to run away. You said so yourself, remember?"

"Not like this!"

"Like what, then? This is how you do it. I know, because I've spent a lot of time thinking about it."

"I bet you have. All this to kidnap me and take me away from my family! It's incredible."

"Come on, Laura, it's not like you'd miss them. They're not normal—they're all a little touched, right?"

Okay, so it probably wasn't a good idea to add a circular motion to the side of my head as I said it. She wasted no time tearing through her bag, taking out the Bic lighter she had brought to the concert, and hurling it at me, striking me in the forehead. There was a dull clunk and I staggered backward. Nice aim, I thought, as good as mine. It hurt, too. Just then a crowd suddenly appeared, and by the time I got over the Bic attack I lost her. I went to the

Women's Restroom and hung out there for as long as I could, but she never came out. I went back to our seats, but she wasn't there, either. I waited through another set, but she still didn't show up. I remembered Enz saying that he and Ronnie were in Section 101, so I went there, too, but no luck. Come to think of it, I didn't see any of them. What was I supposed to do? I was upset about everything: arguing, Bobby Fiore, her lying to me (I guess the "L" really did stand for liar), all the time I had put into the Great Escape, and the fact that everything was coming crashing down like the backdrop in the one-act play the Theatre Dept put on last year. Apparently, somebody had opened a door backstage, which sent a draft of wind upstage, which blew down the forest backdrop (was it an omen?) in the middle of a performance. I thought they were all morons. Now, who's the moron?

I walked around the Spectrum three times, looking for her at each level and even in some of the ramps and stairwells. I started feeling rotten, especially with all of this on-again/off-again, up-down, turn around, put my stomach in knots game that we always play. It was getting to me. A guy can only take so much before he loses his mind and snaps. I wasn't ready to snap, but I was exhausted from looking through crowds of people for her. I went back up to the restaurant level and found a spot where I could rest on a short concrete wall and still see down below without getting hassled by the ushers, which was good, because I needed time to think. As I saw it, there were three possible scenarios: (1) This was a temporary setback and we would get out to Wyoming one way or another, if not in Mr. Andrade's car, then in one "borrowed" from Big Al, (2) The Great Escape was a bust but it accomplished what it was supposed to do, which was bring us closer together, (3) We were finished, kaput, never to see each other again from tonight on. Of all of them, (1) and (3) seemed the least likely because they were the two extremes. I didn't think she'd fall for Wyoming and leaving her family—who knew she would react like that? And (3) didn't make sense even after all of that crap with Bobby Fiore. I could tell

Laura had it bad for me. You just know these things. So that left (2), which meant we would be spending a lot more time together and maybe even get back to the garage.

The concert finally ended after two unbearable encores, thousands of Bic lighters waving from side to side like fireflies in the dark, and I made my way down to the stage area to meet Laura, Enz, and Purple Head. That's when I saw them standing there: Laura, Enz, and Purple Head along with somebody in a fringed suede jacket. I froze, staring at them. They were about to go backstage. I was far enough away to make a hasty exit without being noticed, but Laura caught sight of me and yelled for me to come over. I looked at her, really looked at her: red hair, blue-striped blouse, pink skirt, lips that were beautiful to behold but never really loyal. They couldn't be, not looking like that, not in a million years. All that ever came out of them were lies. Well, she wouldn't have to lie to me anymore, not after tonight. I slowly backed away and let the crowd swallow me up. That was it, all I could feel or remember: Laura staring back at me until we lost sight of each other. And the rest you know.

Saturday, August 14

The next morning I woke to the sound of mom knocking on my door and peeking in, which she hardly ever does, so I figured something was up. It took me a while to open my eyes and adjust to the brightness of the light.

"Richard, get up. It's time to get up. Your teacher is downstairs."

"Teacher?"

"You know, the one whose car you borrowed. Come on, he's waiting."

"What time is it?"

"Eleven."

"Eleven?"

"It comes after ten."

"Be right there."

I got dressed in a hurry, wondering what to tell Mr. Andrade, who was probably pissed that I never returned his car. I guess I would have to tell him the truth. It couldn't hurt. Nobody knew about Wyoming and I hadn't packed anything in the Comet yet, so I was covered there. I could tell him what happened last night without having to lie. This was a first. I kind of liked the idea of not having to cover up. For the past two months I'd been feeling like some sort of spy. It was cool for a while, but now the jig was up.

"Hi, Mister Andrade," I said as I went into the living room. He was sitting with mom, who looked worried.

"Hi, Richard," he mumbled.

There was this stickiness in the air and nobody said anything after that, so I thought I'd get it over with.

"Look, Mister Andrade, I'm really sorry about not returning the car. I got home late and thought about driving it back to school this morning. I guess I overslept."

He looked at me, then mom, then back at me.

"I'm not here about the car, Richard."

"You're not?"

"No. Please, sit down."

I sat in the brown armchair with the ragged arms, embarrassed that he saw how poor we were. Then I realized that my English teacher was actually in our house on a Saturday morning, and I felt even more embarrassed. At least Kornél wasn't around and dad, as usual, was holed up on the third floor, which was a good thing. Mr. Andrade started asking me questions, which I didn't get at all.

"Richard, you didn't leave the concert with Laura last night, did you?"

"No, sir."

"Why not?"

"Well, we got into this argument and she got mad and spent most of the time with her brother. I guess they had backstage passes."

"Enzo?"

"That's right."

"So you left after the concert and they stayed?"

"Yes, to go backstage."

He paused, looking like he had just swallowed a chicken bone. His eyes were bloodshot and for the first time I noticed how old he was. Compared to mom he was much younger, but just then they looked the same age.

"I have some bad news....There was an accident last night," he said.

"An accident?"

"Laura and Enzo left the concert with a third person and were headed up to Temple University, probably to a party. At least that's what the police think."

"Police?"

"Enzo was driving. He has a Corvair, right?"

I nodded.

"Apparently, they were speeding in the rain and spun out at an intersection near Girard Avenue. They hit a parked truck head on. Enzo and Laura were in the front. Enzo died at the scene and Laura an hour later at Saint Joseph's Hospital. The third passenger, who was in the back, is in serious condition. He'll probably pull through."

He stopped, waiting for my reaction, but I just sat there blinking, not really understanding any of it.

"What?"

"Laura's gone, Richard."

"Gone?"

"Yes."

I looked down at the hole in the rug and then up at the drapes and the sunshine coming through the window. I couldn't tell how long it was. I just remember the brightness. It was very bright.

"She was so nice, both of them," mom said. "It's so sad."

I heard the words, but nice and sad were about the only two words in the English language that did not describe Laura, not by a long shot.

"Richard, are you all right?"

I shrugged, I think.

"Say something, will you?"

"Something."

"How do you feel?"

"Nice and sad."

They looked at each other like maybe I had lost my marbles. Then I remembered how Laura had helped me pick up marbles. There was more staring and swallowing and finally mom said, "Maybe I should make some coffee. Would you like some coffee? I can put a pot on. It's fresh."

"Thank you, but I'd better get back to school. The police are investigating the accident and may need me."

He stood up and came over. Then he knelt down and put his hand on my knee. The scene probably looked ridiculous, and I thought of Romeo and Juliet, I don't know why. I laughed, but it didn't throw him off at all. He must have been used to giving teenage death speeches. It sounded like one of those love songs from the 1950s.

"If you ever want to talk about it, let me know. I've left my home number with your mom. Anytime—do you understand that? And don't worry about the car. It can stay here for the time being. Would that be all right?"

I shrugged again but didn't say anything, not even sure I heard right. None of what he said seemed real, especially with his hand on my knee. I wasn't even sure *I* was real. It was possible that I didn't really exist and was just part of the furniture, a fabric covering the armchair. I felt worn like the armchair, so I guess I belonged there. He left after some mumbling and shuffling and both of them staring down at me. Mom turned and said something once the front door was closed, but I couldn't make it out. Did she offer me coffee? I sat there with my arms extended length-wise over the arms of the chair, like snakes mating. I don't know how long that was. Then I went upstairs, got undressed all over again, and curled up in bed. I covered my head with the pillow to keep the glare out. Throughout all of it there was just one thing that kept running through my head over and over and over again. Who was lying in the hospital bed? Who was the third passenger, the survivor? That would tell me everything I needed to know.

Wednesday, August 18
Five Days

I'm in the stands overlooking the football field at St. Rita's. The team is out there practicing and I'm supposed to be working on the story for *The Review*. I didn't want to, but mom thought it would be good for me since I've been in bed for days and never went back to work. Mr. Andrade agreed. So, here I am watching the team and writing in my journal. I've decided to take it with me wherever I go. I guess it's a reminder of Laura, since she's all I ever write about. I want to be able to write in it whenever I feel like it and not have to wait till later. It's also another way of not having to deal with people, cause they're mostly annoying, especially when they come up and stare at me. They don't say anything, just stare like they're at the zoo. I don't even care anymore.

Back on the field, the players move, block, tackle, and run drills, but I don't really see anything. I'm like a camera without film, the shutter opening and closing but nothing happening. The sky is blue, the field is green, the stands are dull silver in the sunlight. There are even birds chirping in the trees, which are leafy and brown. Seems poetic, right? Well, that's exactly how you get fooled. Believe it or not, even birds have an ugly side. The birds in Hitchcock's movie turned on the people in the town just like that.

They even went after that little girl, pulling her hair and scratching her face. See, birds can turn on you. People can turn on you. Life can turn on you. So, don't trust it. Don't trust birds, don't trust people, don't trust life. Don't trust yourself, either, because in the end you don't know what you're capable of doing. I didn't. That's why what happened happened. That's why Laura's not here with me listening to helmets cracking into each other. That's why I'll never look at red hair the same way again, or get into a Corvair, or dream of rubbing myself up against a pair of warm feet that stop my heart cold. I thought this thing with Laura was going to change my life forever. I guess it did.

Monday, August 23
Ten Days

The funeral Mass was at 2:00 pm at Maria Goretti. The church was packed and there were people spilling out of the door onto the sidewalk. It looked like all of St. Rita's was there. All of the Fedoras, too, including Big Al, Rose, who had to be held up by two enormous-looking guys who looked like bullfrogs in three-piece suits, nonno, and the rest of the family dressed in black taking up five rows from the front. A lot of the school people were there: Fr. Augustine Gennaro, the principal, Vice Principal Novak, Mr. Andrade, Mrs. Dudoit, Mr. Ryan, our track coach, and Mrs. Lestor, who was the music teacher and band leader. Of course, Laura's friends were there, a lot with their hair done up and balling like babies, which made me wonder why you would go to a hair salon at a time like this. Most of my friends showed up, guys like Lindeman, Grabowski, and Mike Horowitz, whose father was a Jew and mother Irish. They wore ties and slacks, not the St. Rita colors, though, because we were at Goretti. In the middle of the aisle up front near the altar were two caskets, side by side and covered with white sheets with golden flowers.

There was a television crew from WKBS—Channel 48 in the back. The reporter was a woman with wavy brown hair in a polka-dot blouse with a big bow and vest. I thought it was ironic and maybe Laura's way of telling us that she was still with us, but then the more I thought about it, the more that sounded like a load of crap. I mean, if the reporter was a sign, that meant that what happened was somehow planned by a higher power or at least could have been avoided, but in either case it was no big deal, because Laura had gone to a better place and was waiting for the rest of us to join her. But I didn't buy that. How could I? I didn't care if mom found out, because I was finally growing up, and the first thing I discovered growing up was that everything I believed before was wrong. And not just wrong but the opposite, like up is down, in is out, black is white, on is off. That meant that the worst part of Laura's death wasn't her death at all. It was her betrayal, the betrayal of a "nice" Italian Catholic girl from South Philly. Death you can get over, betrayal you take to your grave. Turns out she was absolutely right about that. I didn't want her to be, but she was, like a lot of things.

I couldn't take all the praying and kneeling and standing, so I got up and moved to the back. I didn't want to be in church, didn't want to be anywhere except bed, which had gotten to be my home while at home, so to speak. But you notice the strangest things and people at times like these. Like Glenn with his glasses and Flute Girl with her braces and Deborah with her butternut breasts, blubbering. Mr. Dudoit was there, too. He didn't look at all the way I pictured him. For one thing, he had a ponytail and an earring, which made me think he really was a Gypsy, so it was good that mom and dad weren't there to argue about it (the air conditioning was on full blast, too). He wore a denim jacket with a black string tie and a silver clasp with a turquoise stone in the middle, which I thought was cool. One of the janitors was there and a couple of the ladies from the cafeteria. I recognized the one who is in charge of the mashed potatoes, green beans, and ginger spice cake, even without the hairnet. I couldn't look at anybody else after that. It was too painful. I also didn't feel like talking to the lone survivor, who was up front in bandages and getting a whole lot of attention. There was a program on a little table in the vestibule like this was a Christmas Pageant with the usual stuff like readings and songs and a thing about the Eucharist for Protestants. I felt pretty sure I wasn't going to repeat my last Eucharistic devotion, and it turned out I was right. There was nothing to get excited about this time, except at the end when this lady as skinny as a pool cue got up and sang Ave Maria by a guy named Gonad or something. It was to be followed by "Testimonials from Family and Friends." That's when I left. I thought about running away for real. Why not? I still had the Cheez-its and the Comet. Everything had been planned. Instead, I walked and walked and just kept walking without looking back. I didn't even know where I was going, but I remembered how I had wished Laura dead and now I couldn't take it back.

Eventually in life you come to a river. I may be 15 ½ but I've figured that much out. So, I passed under 95, crossed South Columbus, and came to the Delaware. I found a trail that went down to the water and followed it to a dock. I took off my jacket and tie, unbuttoned my shirt, which was soaked with sweat, and sat against a tree trunk. It was hot, really hot, and I thought about diving in, but there's one thing I haven't mentioned in all this time writing about my life and opinions. See, I'm a coward. I don't know why, except that I am mostly shy around people, even gentle. Sure, I can talk a big game when I have to, and I've done a lot of it in this journal, but I don't like it when there's shouting and confusion and violence. I don't like violence. But what can you do in high school when you have to beat up or get beaten up? It only takes a couple of times before you learn your lesson. I learned mine, but I am still a coward because I run away from fights. I want to run away from this one, the biggest of my life, except there's nowhere to go. There was nowhere but that dirty river the color of mom's beef broth, and even though the air was throbbing with insects and heat and my shirt was soaked through, there was no way I was diving in. It's funny, too, because when I got home I looked up "Delaware River" and discovered that it's named after the third Baron de la Warr, which is related to "war" and comes from the French *de la Guerre*, which is violence all over again.

I didn't feel like crying, but I missed Laura. I really missed her. I missed her teasing and the way she called me "silly" and how she constantly kept me guessing about whether she liked me or not. Or loved me. I loved her in spite of my jealousy, which made me realize that I finally figured out what love is only after I didn't have it. How screwed up is that? A lot, I'd say. I felt numb, which was a strange way to feel in August. I had to pay attention to my breathing and not get worked up, because if I started to hyperventilate with nobody around, I figured I'd end up dying from asphyxiation (had to look that up, too). So, I sat there looking out at the water, the rusted barge, the bridges (Ben Franklin to the north, Walt Whitman to the south), New Jersey, the Garden State. It wasn't too exciting, just a lot of nothing happening and the sun moving a couple of degrees and maybe a splash in the water. Fish or wave? And the nonstop slapping of waves against the greasy piles.

It's been ten days. Ten days without Laura. Laura Fedora. I guess I've gone longer than that without seeing her, but this time was different. Before, I knew I'd see her again even with all my bitching and making up the Great Question and going on and on about love. That's just what I do: go on and on about things I know nothing about even when I've got no reason to bitch. See, I knew I'd see Laura again and that things would work out (scenario 2). I did all that complaining and theorizing because it gave me something to do, brought us closer together (much better than Seals and Crofts), and was fun. Yeah, it was fun writing about things I felt and imagined. It was beyond anything I've ever done in school, even with parabolic functions and crap like that. Actually, the most exciting part about schoolwork is getting a new textbook and smelling the spine for the first few weeks. My history text was terrific that way, smelled like vanilla and glue and had glossy pages that you could glide your hand across and thump your fingers on.

But it's different now. She's not at home on the phone or working on a story for *The Review* or looking for trees to kiss under. Ten days without her isn't like ten days with her. Knowing that, if I wanted to, I could sit in her kitchen with nonno and wait for her to come skipping down the stairs was a comfort, even when I wasn't sure how she felt about me, when things were still up in the air between us. They're not in the air anymore, but that's the tragedy. Isn't that what tragedy is—finally getting what you want only to find out it doesn't matter anymore? I don't know. But what's the point of loving a dead person? Please, tell me. Does it matter to anybody? Maybe to Rose and the Fedoras, in their crazy way. They get to go home and cry and yell at each other and do whatever it is they do. But what am I supposed to do? Where can I go? How do I go back to being a stupid high school kid whose life is track practice and tubes of zit cream?

Ten days. I'll tell you something, I don't know how I made it this long. It's a lot harder than the first ten minutes or ten hours, because it's just about the time you run out of excuses for sitting down and thinking about what happened and why. Not that that ever really happened to me, because that's all I've been thinking about, which is why I spent so much time in bed. I'd get up once in a while to take a piss or stare out the window. A couple of times I worked on the drawings in this journal. I'm not an artist, but I wanted them to look their very best, even the toilet bowl. It's the simpler things that take the longest time.

"Wow. That's so profound, Merk, why don't you put it in a fortune cookie?" I can hear her say.

"Why don't you put *this* in a fortune cookie?"

"Hey, it'd probably fit."

I laughed, because it was funny and just like something she'd say, but it wasn't mean, which is something I have to explain, because it might be on your mind. It was on mine for the longest time, her being cruel and all. But it's not like that. I know it's freakin bizarre of me to say, especially after everything that's happened and what I just wrote, but it's true. Laura wasn't like that, and the reason I know is that she was just like me. Let's face it, her cruelty to me was just like mine to Kornél. Neither one of us meant it, wasn't what we wanted to do, but was part of who we were. I see that now. Maybe the best way I can explain it is the time I had to paint the garage door and ran out of paint. Instead of going back to the hardware store (cause it's a whole four blocks away), I mixed some white trim paint I found in the basement with the green outdoor paint for the garage. It made just enough to finish the garage without my having to go to the store again. Mom loved it, dad approved, and I never told anyone that the green had streaks of white in it. In fact, I could see the white streaks as I mixed both paints together and stirred them. Looking at it, you'd never know the green had white in it. Looking at Laura (or me), you'd never know there were streaks of cruelty mixed in either one of us, but there they were. So, honestly, how can I blame her without blaming myself?

I sat there for the longest time trying to figure it all out, but it was too damn hot. I got back to Maria Goretti sometime after four. By then, just about everybody had cleared out and gone to the cemetery, including the TV crew. I came across Lindeman in the parking lot, smoking a joint with Horowitz.

"Where you been?" he said, his face red.

"Went for a walk. What the hell are you guys doing smoking weed in a church parking lot?"

"It's the safest place. Nobody's around."

"Want some?" Horowitz asked.

I'd never done it before, never really wanted to, but I figured there were a lot of firsts happening. Anyway, it was part of growing up.

"Sure," I said. It felt harsh going down. I coughed. They laughed.

"Come on, let's go for ice cream," Lindeman said.

"I should go home."

"No, ice cream."

"Hey, Tommy, it's a fucking funeral," Horowitz reminded hm.

"Oh, yeah, right."

So they drove me home, but I heard them talking up front about a new frozen yogurt place on Spring Garden. When I got inside, I went upstairs without saying a word to anyone, even mom when she asked me how it went (*it was a fucking funeral, mom*), and went straight to bed.

Saturday, August 28
Fifteen Days

So now I'm not eating, at least that's what they tell me. But I don't feel like eating, except when I meet Horowitz and we smoke half a joint before going out for yogurt or to Dairy Queen. You'd think I'd be obese but I'm not. I sleep a lot, and mom is worried. They even sent me to a therapist, this hippie with frizzy hair and a Golden Retriever that sits by her side during our sessions. I think she meets dad's definition of Gypsy. Anyway, "Marsha" told me to write a letter to Laura to get everything out, the happy, the sad, the things that make sense, the things that don't, the incongruous (her word), the things that confuse me, and how I feel abandoned by Laura. Okay, so I did. It actually beats talking to an empty chair and is more fitting for a moody writer. Honestly, though, I don't think I want to be a writer anymore. It's too much work and way too painful. I don't want to think about how I feel or feel what I think or whatever. I'd rather not think or feel anything. That's just the way it is.

All right, so here's my letter. After this, I am going to retire, figure out something else to do. Who knows, maybe teach Latin to underprivileged kids in the Bronx or someplace. I ask you to read it and not make fun of it or correct the grammar or anything. Just finish the letter and put the journal down, in storage would be good, padlocked. It's been nice talking to you, reader, but summer is over...Gone...I'm done with it.

A Letter for Laura

Hi, Laura. I'm writing to you, because I'm supposed
to tell you how I feel and how much I miss you and all.
It's not that I don't want to do it or feel those things.
It's just that it feels phony and probably not what you
want to hear, so I'm thinking why bother? But then
that sounds like I'm lazy or don't care, which I am
not. I mean, I haven't had a whole lot of energy lately
(no running or anything like that, although coach says
it'll good do me good), but I am not lazy about writing
to you and can prove it, because I spent all summer
writing about you in my journal, which is where I
am writing this letter. I never told you that, but it's
the truth. It's not like I'm going to mail it, though,
so Marsha said the journal would be fine. She's my
shrink, although she doesn't want me to call her
that, because she doesn't want to shrink my mind
but expand it and my passion for life. Her words, not
mine, which you can probably tell.

I don't have a passion for life right now. I guess it's
because I had a passion for you and now you're gone.
I don't really want to do anything except sleep and
smoke weed with my friend Mike. If mom ever found
out she'd probably have a heart attack and send me
to live with relatives in Hungary, which would be pretty
bad what with them being Communists and all. So I
have to sneak around to do it. I know you wouldn't
approve, but it's like the only thing I look forward
to and makes me feel good. I've thought a couple of
times about going over to your parents' house, but I
wouldn't know what to say, especially to your mom.
I heard she's still taking sleeping pills and never gets
out of bed. I understand that, believe me. I could buy

some grapefruit and take nonno for a walk in the park, but he might not want that and get all mixed up.

It's lonely here without you, mainly because I don't have anything worthwhile to do and no one to do it with. I can't talk to the guys about you, I can't talk to mom, and dad is busy trying to finish his Variable design that is supposed to make us a ton of money. Maybe with my share I can travel to Wyoming for both of us. I wouldn't sleep in a tree house or anything like that. Probably get a nice hotel room with velvet drapes and order a cappuccino with biscotti. But I think I'd just end up sleeping all day. There'd be no point to doing anything, really. It's no fun doing things by myself. I've figured out that the biggest thing about love is not having some grand experience or even getting your world turned upside down, which you did to mine with your red hair and painted toenails and eyes that saw right through me. It's not even about your nipples or derriere, honest to God. See, I've figured out that the biggest thing about love is having somebody to do things with, to share your life with. If you don't have anybody, then the biggest thing you could do like walk on the moon wouldn't seem like such a big deal, while the smallest thing like frying an egg would be terrific if you could do it with somebody you love. I don't know what made me think of that except that mom tries to feed me fried eggs all the time to keep my protein level up.

What I want to say is that my life won't ever be the same without you. You made me feel things I never felt before, like electricity was running through my veins. Nothing else felt as important as seeing you, and now that I can't do that anymore, it feels like I've got a hole in me, like somebody shot me (for real this time). I don't think that hole is ever going to be filled. I guess I should say thank you for the time we had together (that's what everybody tells me), but, to tell you the truth, I feel like I've been robbed. I can't help it. I don't feel anything noble or religious, just a lot of pain. I watched that red fern movie the other night, you know the one where one of the dogs dies and the other one sits on the grave for days until it dies from grief. Well, that's just how I feel now. I'm going to sit on your grave until they chase me away or I drop dead.

I also wanted to tell you I'm really sorry about all the arguing and doubting you and even hating you. I hated you that night at the concert. I guess that was my fault, cause I can get jealous and pretty uptight when I think somebody's pushing me around, whether it was you or him. I promise I will not get jealous or uptight about things like that ever again, not that I'll ever be with anybody ever again. I can't imagine find-ing anybody who could do to me what you did--make me feel like the moment I saw you I was ready to die. Seriously, I was ready to die and wasn't worried one bit about being swallowed up by death or hell or anything. Who else could do that to me? Who? At least we had those moments in the garage and in Mr. Andrade's office when we first met. I was the happiest guy on the planet. Can a 15 ½-year-old dude say that? No, but I can. I don't care what anybody else says about teenage love or bubblegum romance or hormones, I know the truth. With you I was ready to die--cross my heart! I didn't hope for it, but that's what happened. So now I'll just spend the rest of my life waiting to catch up to you. Wait for me, okay? I don't know what else to say except I love you with everything *inside* of me. *Outside*, too, you know.

Merk

It was late afternoon by the time Richard closed the journal and set it down on the wall next to him. He hadn't looked up in hours. He did so now only to find Junior gone and the sun melting in the west over Guatemala. He stared blankly as a gull cried overhead, hardly noticing. It was strange that he hadn't remembered any of that summer until now, none of the anguish and longing not only over losing Laura, but over his own family. He hadn't thought of his father as a young man, an inventor with a sense of humor and dread of failure similar to his own, but there it was in black and white, with illustrations. Was it that dread that had condemned both of them? The thing he feared the most, that his father feared the most, had come to pass. He had lost everything dear to him, and the beginning of the end had happened when he was young. He had given up hope, not fighting for Laura but letting her go, letting her slip into the swamp of her own ego and need for rebellion. Maybe if he had gone up to her that night instead of turning and running away, she would have lived. He also never realized that his cynicism had started so early. He supposed that it had been more recent, something from law school or marriage, which would have made it, if not less painful, at least more understandable. But his had started much earlier, as did his awareness of his own sexuality. It was obvious that he had been a horny teenager, which pleased him even now. At least he had been precocious in that department. Not a complete failure there.

But it wasn't any of that that had made him sit in silence until the guard called him for dinner. It was Merk, the boy who had tried to find his way through life mainly on his own, as if learning to walk through love and sex and his own soul, not sure where to go or whom to trust. Had Norm Fay been right in helping him plan his Great Escape, or was he some sort of deviant who couldn't hold a job? Did it really matter? Merk had needed him then, or at least someone like him to guide him through a world of self-doubt and confusion. And the guy had come through, red shoes and all. He had helped a kid in need and even warned him about that night in 1976. That was no small feat. And that was exactly what Richard needed to do now: help a kid in need. The kid was himself, a young version of Richard Mercurius. Merk needed Richard's help, which was something he had needed all along but had been denied him. Now, it was time. It might be just the thing that the older version needed as well. That thought was a comfort as Richard got up and walked into the jail with the red journal under his arm. After all, he was much older now and ready to fight back.